RAINMAKER WITCH

MISS MATCHED MIDLIFE DATING AGENCY
BOOK FIVE

DEANNA CHASE

ABOUT THIS BOOK

There's never a dull moment in Premonition Pointe for Marion Matched, full-time midlife matchmaker and part-time bad guy butt-kicker for the local Magical Task Force.

With her boyfriend Jax busy learning how to deal with his own paranormal abilities, Marion focuses on rebuilding her recently sabotaged business—the matchmaking one, not the butt-kicking one. Which means when a new wolf pack moves into town, Marion agrees to help the charismatic alpha find his mate. Only when Premonition Pointe residents begin to vanish, and everyone in town, including the local law enforcement, blame the new wolves, she finds herself right in the middle of another controversy.

Convinced the pack isn't to blame, Marion takes matters into her own hands. And when a loved one turns up on the missing list, Marion will stop at nothing to find them and to take down the person who is terrorizing the people of her beloved town.

CHAPTER 1

"*Y*ou have a whisker in the middle of your forehead," Charlotte said in a matter-of-fact tone as she tied her long red hair up into a messy bun.

I jerked my head up and stared at her. "What?"

"You heard me, Bigfoot," my sister said as she tapped something into her computer.

"Bigfoot?" I gasped out, offended.

Charlotte threw her head back and cackled. "If the hairy beast description fits…"

"People don't grow whiskers out of their foreheads, Charlotte," I spat as I jumped out of my office chair and ran to the adjoining bathroom.

"You do!" she called after me.

I quickly checked and found a two-inch-long hair that was so pale and fine it was barely visible. Though Charlotte *had* seen it from ten feet away. Since she'd just gotten glasses for nearsightedness, suddenly I had to concede that Bigfoot might have been an apt nickname. With a groan, I pulled out my emergency tweezers and plucked the offending hair. Then I checked the rest of my face, making sure I wasn't sporting a collection of whiskers. When I was satisfied I wasn't growing a five-o'clock-shadow, I slipped back into the office and sat heavily at my desk. "I swear to the goddess, perimenopause is the worst."

"Is that what you think the issue is with your sudden ability to grow hair everywhere?" Charlotte asked.

"Yes. One hundred percent. So that's something you can look forward to," I quipped, making sure she knew she'd be dealing with the same thing someday.

"Please. I don't have to worry about that for what, twenty years? I'm sure by then we'll have plenty of advancements in aesthiology, so I won't have to deal with" —she waved her hand at me—"whatever you have going on."

I rolled my eyes at her and flopped back into my chair.

Charlotte peered at me and then smirked. "Honestly, I figured it was just a side effect from getting it on with your werewolf boyfriend."

I raised both eyebrows. "How so?"

"You know, sharing DNA. I figured that was enough to make you a little hairier. Now that he's a shifter, I did sort of wonder if it made him hairier now. Please tell me he doesn't have back fur when he's in his human form now."

"You're ridiculous," I said, unable to stifle my laugh. "No, he doesn't have back fur now." At least I didn't think he did. It felt like forever since I'd set eyes on my boyfriend, Jax Williams. After an unfortunate encounter with a werewolf, he'd been bitten and infected with the werewolf curse. He was now off with my previously-assumed-dead, former best friend, Trish, who also happened to be a werewolf shifter, and he was learning how to deal with living as a shapeshifting werewolf.

My chest ached with loneliness at the thought of Jax. It had only been six weeks since he'd left town, but since I didn't know when he was coming back, each day only made the wait seem a million times longer. I let out a quiet sigh and went back to working on an ad to try to bring in more business. After our client, Sara, had been accused of attempting to murder all the dates I'd set up for her, the business had taken a serious hit. Nobody wanted to work with a dating agency that had repped a murderer. Even though the charges were dropped and Sara was exonerated, there was still a public stigma. And if we didn't do something soon, I wasn't sure we'd be able to keep the doors open.

"That's good. I don't think I could deal with someone who had a rug on their back. Think of the waxing bill." She peered at me. "Speaking of waxing, you should probably make a spa appointment soon. You don't want to be sporting that mustache when Jax gets back in town. Some highlights would probably do you good, too."

My hand flew to my upper lip, and when all I felt was the smooth skin from my last waxing, I picked up the stress ball that was lying on my desk and threw it at her. Though she had a point about the highlights. Or hell, it might be time to go for a full dye job. I hadn't missed the hints of gray peeking through my own red strands of hair when I'd been inspecting the offending facial hair just moments ago.

My much younger sister was too busy cackling at her

own joke to notice the ball, and it bounced off her forehead, making her laugh even harder.

"You're the worst," I said, shaking my head.

"You love me." She winked and then threw the stress ball back at me.

I caught it easily with my left hand just as the office door opened.

"Hey, you," Carly Preston said, poking her head in. "You busy?"

"Never too busy for you," I said, rising to greet her.

The down-to-earth movie star pushed the door open and swept in with an equally gorgeous and famous television star on her heels.

"Autumn," I said with a pleased smile as I headed straight for her to shake her hand. "It's a pleasure to finally get you into the office."

"The pleasure is all mine," she said, her easy smile reaching her bright blue eyes. "You know I've been wanting to do this for a while now. Plus Carly can't stop talking about you and your agency. I figured it was time to make good on that promise I made to check it out."

"Only good things, I hope," I said, relief rushing through me. Autumn was a well-known television star and getting her on board to try out and promote the dating agency was just the thing we needed to turn this business around.

Carly laughed. "Of course, only good things." She walked over and took a seat in front of my desk and waved for Autumn to follow her.

"Sorry I had to reschedule so many times," Autumn said. "With opening the pottery shop, I've had a lot on my plate."

"No need to apologize," I said quickly. "I'm just thrilled

you're here at all. Can I get you ladies anything? Coffee? Tea? Water?"

"Coffee would be great," Carly said, looking lovely in her cream blouse and flowing navy-blue linen pants. From her freshly dyed blond hair down to her cream-colored stilettos, she looked every inch old Hollywood. "Black."

"Make that two," Autumn added as she took a seat next to Carly. The television star was dressed casually in jeans and a form fitting T-shirt, and I couldn't help but notice the clay stains around her cuticles. But she still had that fresh glow that all famous actors seemed to possess. She gave me a tired smile as she added, "That cup I had just after five this morning is long gone now."

"Five?" Charlotte gasped out. "That's unholy."

I cleared my throat and gave my sister an annoyed look as I shook my head slightly, indicating her input wasn't welcome, and then walked over to the coffee maker and got to work.

Autumn just chuckled. "I used to say that, too, but these days, I get my best work done early in the morning. Gotta get on it before my brain turns to mush in the afternoon."

"You noticed that, too?" Carly asked her. "I swear, if I don't finish my work by four, I'm a bumbling mess for the rest of the afternoon and evening. I even used to be a night owl, getting my best work hours in while everyone else was sleeping. Those days are long gone."

"Getting old sounds miserable," a familiar voice said from behind me.

I swallowed a groan as I glanced back at Celia, my resident ghost.

"Thank the goddess I'll never have to worry about that

or saggy boobs," she quipped as she floated closer to Charlotte, her long blond hair flying out behind her.

"Sure, no saggy boobs, but no one will be able to touch them either," Charlotte said helpfully. "I'm not sure I'd want to give up sexy times just for eternally great skin."

Carly and Autumn laughed while I braced myself for the backlash. If there was one thing Celia hated about being a ghost, it was that she'd never again get to indulge in the pleasures of the flesh.

"That was just rude," Celia practically snarled at Charlotte. "Besides, Danny and I get up to plenty of fun. You ever heard of phone sex?"

"You talk to your ghost boyfriend on the phone?" Charlotte asked, raising one eyebrow.

Celia widened her Kewpie doll eyes. "Oh. Em. Gee. No, I—"

"That's enough!" I held my hands up. "We don't need to hear about all that. This is a place of business after all."

"It's a dating agency, Marion," my sister said with a chuckle. "If we can't talk about sex here, where can we?"

I ignored her and turned to Autumn. "I'm so sorry. I wish I could say this isn't normal, but when you have a resident ghost with no filter, there's just no controlling things."

Autumn laughed. "Honestly, after being alone in my studio all week, this is quite the refreshing change." She glanced at Celia. "You have a boyfriend?"

Celia's smile widened. "Yep. We met at the *Abs, Buns, and Guns* show. He used to work there before his untimely death."

Autumn's lips twitched with amusement. "He was one of the dancers?"

"As a matter of fact, he was," Celia said, straightening as a look of pride washed over her. "You should come down sometime and meet him. He's still the most gorgeous guy in the place."

"Maybe for the next girls' night out," Carly said with a nod.

I grimaced, unable to imagine what would happen if the two Hollywood stars walked into the male strip club. No doubt the paparazzi would be all over it and the internet would go crazy. I cleared my throat. "Um, maybe we should shelve that idea for the moment. You're obviously free to do whatever you wish, and while I personally have no problem with male strippers, I'm not sure attending a strip club while looking for your soul mate is the message we want to send with this campaign."

Both Carly and Autumn started laughing. Carly laughed so hard that tears started to stream down her face. She sucked in a sharp breath and wheezed out, "You're right, Marion."

I blinked at her, wondering what was so hilarious.

"You have no idea how right you are," Autumn got out between giggles.

"What is wrong with them?" Celia asked me, sounding confused. "Strip clubs aren't that funny."

When Carly finally caught her breath, she wiped her eyes and said, "Autumn owes her success in television to Mika Malone. Ever heard of her?"

I shook my head.

"Right. She was slated to star in *My Witchy Life* as the sweet and naive Bianca Bellflower until she was caught on camera, clearly drunk with a cigarette in her hand as she stumbled into Peter Piper's Fantasy Palace in West Hollywood. The network cut her immediately, and that's how Autumn got the role."

"That's… terrible for Mika," I said, knowing that if the situation were reversed and that had been a man going into an adult entertainment establishment, it would have been covered up immediately.

"Yes it was," Autumn agreed. "But she was a back-stabbing bitch who slept with my boyfriend at the time, so I didn't feel too badly about taking that part."

"She also sold lies to the tabloids about anyone she saw as competition, including me," Carly said. "So don't think less of us if our compassion appears to be in the toilet."

"Screw Mika," I said as a sudden rush of disgust washed over me. Clearly Mika had gotten what she deserved.

"I do think those morality clauses in the Hollywood contracts are ridiculous, but I can see why the studio wanted someone with a wholesome reputation for Bianca," Carly said. "The success of the show would have been in jeopardy if she'd been seen as a party girl."

I could see that. *My Witchy Life* was a sweet family show that had dominated the airwaves for over a decade and was still very popular on a notable streaming network.

"Okay, so no strip clubs until after the campaign?" I said with a smirk.

"Let's be honest," Autumn said with a chuckle. "I'm not likely to ever make it to the strip club, but I'll be sure to be on my best behavior."

"Borrrrring," Celia said and then vanished from the office.

"She's fun," Autumn said.

"She is... usually," I agreed. She was also great at keeping an eye on anyone I needed to keep tabs on and had been a lifesaver when we'd been hunting down bad guys. Who knew having a ghost around all the time would prove to be so helpful? I tapped my computer, making it come to life. "Let's get started. What kind of man are you looking for?"

Autumn pursed her lips, indicating that she was thinking. "Someone accomplished. I don't mean he has to be rich or anything. Just someone who isn't threatened by my past success. You'd be amazed at how many men have such fragile egos that they can't stand it when I'm recognized or am invited to exclusive events because of my former life as an actress. I need someone who can handle that without acting like a manbaby."

"Absolutely," I said, jotting that down, though I really didn't need to. It was my mission to find my clients self-confident partners who celebrated their successes. "Any physical preferences? Age range? What don't you like in a partner?"

"Hmm." She leaned forward. "I tend to go for long and lean runner types, but I'm open to any physique. Typically, I find myself attracted to smart men who have a great sense of humor. Self-confidence is sexy, but arrogance isn't. And he has to love dogs."

We chatted a bit more until I was sure I had a good handle on what type of person Autumn was looking for, and then I told her, "This is good. Let me go through my client list and see who I think might be a good fit, and then I'll give you a call."

"Perfect." Autumn stood. "Anything else?"

"We're going to need to set up a photoshoot," Charlotte said. "And I'll need you to sign a release that says we can use your image in our social media posts and ad campaign."

I stared at my sister, marveling at her professionalism. When had she turned into such a pro? She hadn't worked with me for very long, but in those weeks, she'd gone from filing her nails on a daily basis to this person, who was clear-eyed and ready to start our next online campaign.

"Sure." Autumn and Charlotte took care of the nitty gritty while I chatted with Carly about the next coven meeting.

"Next Tuesday is the full moon," Carly said. "Grace wants to do a cleansing ritual. She said she's had too much questionable juju lately. Apparently, she's had three escrows fall through in the past month, and she thinks she picked up some bad energy from an asshole client."

"Oof, okay. We'll cleanse her energy then."

Autumn glanced at us. "Is this a closed coven meeting, or are random witches invited?"

Carly rolled her eyes. "Random witches? No. But you? Yes. Definitely. I'll pick you up on the way."

I smiled at her, happy to be including another witch. It wasn't that long ago when the Premonition Pointe coven had welcomed me as one of their own. As far as I was concerned, the more witches the better.

"Okay, we're done here," Charlotte said. "I'll give you a call about the photoshoot."

"Sounds good." Autumn held her hand out to me. "It was

a pleasure to finally get the ball rolling on this. I look forward to finding out who you select for me."

"Likewise." I walked them to the door, but just before they left, there was a knock. I blinked at Charlotte. "Are we expecting anyone?"

"Nope," she said with a shake of her head.

I pulled the door open and found a tall, handsome man with piercing green eyes. "Hi there. Can I help you?"

"Are you Marion?" he asked in a deep voice that was even sexier than I could have imagined.

"Yes," I said as I glanced at Autumn, who was staring at him intently.

"Good. You're just the person I was looking for," the man said. "I hear you're the best matchmaker on the West Coast."

"That's flattering." I smiled at him.

His gaze flicked to Autumn, and I felt rather than saw an electric connection between them. I glanced at my sister, desperately wishing she was standing next to me so I could see their auras together.

As if Charlotte could read my mind, she hurried over to me and placed a hand on my arm. Immediately, both of their auras lit up and merged into a glorious shade of deep violet.

"Well, this is interesting," Charlotte said under her breath.

I cleared my throat and turned my attention back to the man. "And you are?"

He held his hand out. "Kai Gray, pack leader of the Diablo Wolf Pack."

CHAPTER 2

"*L*eader of a wolf pack," Autumn said, looking intrigued. "What brings you to Premonition Pointe?"

Kai cast his mysterious gaze on her, and I couldn't help but notice the appreciation flash through those eyes. He gave her a devastating smile. "Wine. Gray Wolf Winery to be exact. And what do you do here in town?"

Autumn glanced away nervously but then quickly returned her gaze to his, looking a little flushed. "I own a pottery studio and gallery. It's just a few doors down."

"A pottery studio, huh? I'll have to check it out."

My mind was racing as I watched the wolf and the former television star flirt shamelessly. Kai was a leader of a wolf pack? Was that Trish's pack? Did that mean Jax was nearby? I was dying to ask the man but held my tongue, trying to stay professional in front of my new client. "Mr. Gray, why don't you have a seat at my desk while I walk these ladies out? And then I can give you my full attention and discuss how I can help you."

"Right this way," Charlotte said, taking him by the arm and leading him toward my desk.

I hurried Autumn and Carly out the door and said my goodbyes, promising to call as soon as I had a game plan.

Autumn eyed the closed door. "That man, Kai? He's exactly my type. Tall, thin but muscular. You know… just in case you needed a visual."

I raised one eyebrow. "You want me to set you up with Kai?"

"Well, I didn't say that exactly." Her cheeks flushed deep maroon. "Dating a werewolf seems… problematic. But he's definitely hot."

Celia appeared right next to me. "You said before you want a man who likes dogs. Seems like a wolf would fit that bill," she said with a giggle.

"Celia!" I admonished even as I wanted to laugh. Autumn had indicated she was a dog lover.

Autumn rolled her eyes, but her lips twitched with amusement. "You have a point, but I'm just sticking my toe back into the dating pool. I'm not sure I'm ready for someone who howls at the moon."

Carly cackled, and the two of them waved their goodbyes as they left the building.

"She has no idea what she's missing," Celia said and then disappeared again.

I vaguely wondered when Celia had experienced dating a werewolf and then shook my head, trying to dislodge the thought. There was no telling with that one.

Anxious to find out if Kai had any news about Jax, I

hurried back into the office to find my sister half-sitting on my desk, curling a lock of hair with her finger and making moon eyes at the man. Walking over, I cleared my throat and then nodded toward her desk. "I've got it from here, Charlotte."

My sister gave me an irritated flat stare before standing and smiling down at Kai. "Let me know if you need anything. Anything at all."

Kai chuckled softly as my sister sashayed her way to her desk.

I settled in my chair and leaned forward, my hands clasped. "Before we get started, can I ask if you know Jax Williams?"

His amused expression turned serious. "Yes, actually. That's why I decided to come check out your service. I figured anyone who is dating a wolf must not have reservations about taking one on as a client."

Relief washed over me, and suddenly the tension in my shoulders eased. "So he is with your pack? How is he doing?"

Kai nodded. "He's... still working out how to deal with his new reality. It's not an easy task."

"Yes, that's what Trish said. I just want to know that he's okay."

"He is doing as well as can be expected," he said, his expression unreadable. "It can take months, sometimes years for adults to adjust to their new wolf status. I know it's hard to be patient when you're missing a loved one, but the best thing you can do for him right now is to just wait for him to contact you. He will when he's ready."

Right. It was pretty much what Jax had asked of me when

he'd left all those weeks ago. He'd just wanted time. But how much time? Months? Years? *No*, my mind screamed. There was no way my Jax, wolf or not, would disappear for years. He'd find a way back to me one way or another. I knew it in my gut.

Determined to put my melancholy behind me and be the professional I knew myself to be, I said, "Okay, Kai Gray. Why don't you tell me more about yourself and what kind of partner you're looking for?"

His lips twitched into a small smile of approval as he placed his elbows on his knees and gave me his full attention. "As I said before, I'm the Alpha of the Diablo Wolf Pack. The pack recently purchased a small private winery on the north side of town on Pointe Meadow Road along with some adjacent land. My intension is to make the winery a bit of a destination spot with a farm-to-table restaurant, a luxury spa, and possible music venue. I want the winery to be the go-to event space for weddings, family reunions, and all other celebrations. We don't want to be just another business in town, we want to be part of the fabric of Premonition Pointe as we lay down roots for our pack members. Part of that foundation for me is finding someone to settle down with who isn't already part of the pack. I need someone who sees me as an equal and not their pack leader."

I sat back in my chair, more than a little surprised by his speech. "Wolves put down roots?" I asked without thinking.

Storm clouds rolled through his piercing eyes as he pressed his lips into an impatient thin line. "Yes, Miss Matched. Wolves put down roots. What did you think we did? Run from forest to forest, ravaging everything in sight until we'd depleted all the resources?"

"I..." I shook my head, feeling foolish. "No. Of course not." The truth was that my best friend had turned into a wolf and gone into hiding for years. And for some reason, I'd gotten it in my head that wolves were roamers. That they stayed on the move, but that was because of my limited experience. It wasn't every day that a girl ran into a werewolf. Or at least most girls. I just happened to now have three of them in my life. "I apologize if I offended you, Mr. Gray."

Kai's tight expression vanished. "You didn't. Not really. It's just that wolves are prone to even more stereotypes than witches. I try to fight them where I can."

I couldn't help but let out a laugh. He had me there. Witches did suffer all sorts of stereotypes among those who didn't have power. I could only imagine it was a hundred times worse for a man who shifted into a completely different creature. "Fair enough. So you're looking for a partner. Someone to lead your pack with you?" If he wanted a wolf partner, this was certainly going to be a challenge.

"No," he said, shaking his head slightly. "Not to lead the pack. The other wolves won't follow anyone but their Alpha. What I mean is someone who is an equal in both my personal and professional life."

"So someone who could run the winery with you?" I started jotting down notes.

"Yes, someone who *could* run the winery, but not necessarily someone who wants to." His green eyes sparked with amusement. "In other words, I want someone intelligent enough that they could do it, but I'm not necessarily looking for a business partner."

"You want someone you can bounce ideas off and who will challenge you," I said, reading between the lines. "You're not interested in anyone who is overly impressed with you or is happy to sit back and let you make all the decisions."

"Exactly." He sat back in his chair, studying me. "I can see why you have a reputation for being the best matchmaker."

"I've been doing this a long time, Mr. Gray. Cutting through the bullshit and getting down to brass tacks is pretty much my specialty. Now, two more questions."

"Shoot."

"Do you have a preference on physical type? And does she need to be a shifter?"

Kai glanced at the door quickly and then back at me. "Athletic. Age appropriate. Definitely not a shifter."

"What did you think of Autumn?" Charlotte called.

"Autumn?" Kai asked me.

"The pretty blonde you were talking to when you first arrived," I said, shooting my sister a look meant to shut her up.

"I don't tend to pick women on looks alone, but I wouldn't turn down drinks with either of those women," he said.

"Carly is taken," Charlotte added helpfully.

"Thank you, Charlotte," I snapped and then gave Kai a smile. "I think I have enough to go on. All we need to do is fill out some paperwork, and then I'll get started on finding you some matches." I stood and held out my hand. "It's been a pleasure to meet you, Mr. Gray."

"It's Kai." He wrapped his fingers around mine. His skin was slightly rough, making me suspect he spent most days working with his hands. His touch reminded me of Jax, and I couldn't help the ache of loneliness as I wondered, yet again, when I'd see him.

CHAPTER 3

"*J*'m headed out. Denver is taking me to dinner and then a movie," Charlotte said, glancing at me and her dog, who was sitting next to me on the couch. "Can you take care of Minx if I don't make it back home tonight?"

"Sure," I said, happy to have a little bit of company even if it was a small Chihuahua dressed in the tiniest daisy-print dress. At least I wouldn't be wallowing alone. If anyone missed Jax more than me, it was Minx. The little creature had formed a freakish bond with him over the past months and had taken to standing by the door every evening, hoping that Jax would appear.

"Thanks." Charlotte bent down and kissed Minx on the head before sweeping her gaze over me. "Try to do something other than eat ice cream and watch *Teen Wolf* again, okay? It's getting a little pathetic."

"*Teen Wolf* is the perfect movie," I said, ignoring her jab about the ice cream. If I wanted to skip dinner for my favorite chocolate caramel swirl, that was my prerogative.

"If you say so. See ya later." She swept out of the house, leaving me and Minx staring at each other.

"Are you ready for treats, sweet girl?" I asked her.

Minx jumped off the couch and ran into the kitchen, waiting impatiently next to the treat drawer.

I laughed. "I was going to put my jammies on first, but this is what I get for mentioning the T word, right?" After nearly getting the tips of my fingers chomped off by Minx the monster, I let out a yelp and said, "That was rude, even for you, little girl."

Minx ignored my admonishment and ran into the other room. I let out a sigh, slipped into my bedroom to put on my pajamas, and then went for the freezer. Moments later, I was curled up on the couch with a pint of ice cream in one hand and the remote in the other. As I was digging my spoon into the chocolate caramel swirl, there was a knock on the door followed by someone walking in.

"Ty, is that you?" I asked, not bothering to look away from the television. Ty, the young man I thought of as a son, lived in my garage apartment with his partner, Kennedy.

"Surprise," a familiar woman's voice said cheerily.

I jerked and twisted around to see Trish, my former best friend and Ty's biological mother, striding toward me with a bouquet of sunflowers in her hand. "Trish, what are you doing here?"

She walked past me and right into the kitchen as if she owned the place. "Bringing you flowers. What does it look like?"

Her words were normal enough, but her voice had a

high-pitched tone that told me she was nervous. As she should be. Trish and I had been as close as sisters once. Or at least I'd thought we were. But then she'd faked her death, leaving Ty and I grieving for her for years. While she done it under a misguided attempt to protect us from her psychotic ex, Ty and I were having trouble forgiving her for not trusting us.

While Trish and I were trying to work on our relationship, we were *not* at the point where just walking in unannounced was appreciated. Still, she'd brought me flowers, and I wasn't sure I wanted any sort of confrontation.

Trish brought the vase of flowers in from the kitchen and set them on the coffee table. "There. They really add cheer to the place, don't you think?"

Minx jumped toward her, growling.

Trish jerked back and glared at the dog. "What did I ever do to you?"

"She's just doing her job, Trish," I said, not bothering to hide my impatience. "Minx doesn't know you and she's just protecting me."

"Well, can you call her off? I can't sit if she's keeping me trapped on this side of the table."

"Minx, it's okay," I said. "Come here."

The little dog gave Trish one last growl and then eyed her as she slowly made her way back to my side. Without looking up, I asked, "How's Jax?"

Trish hesitated for a long moment before answering. "He's on his journey."

I jerked my head up, staring her down. "What kind of answer is that?"

"The only one I can give." Trish let out a long sigh and leaned against the frame of the wide opening that led to the kitchen. "Each wolf has a different journey. You'll hear from him when he's ready."

"So you're not even going to tell me if you've seen him?" I demanded.

"I've seen him," she finally conceded. "But not since he hooked up with a new pack—"

"The Diablo pack," I said, cutting her off.

"How did you—"

"I met Kai Gray this morning. He confirmed that he knows Jax."

"Yeah. Kai is an acquaintance of mine. I introduced them," she said.

I frowned at my friend. "But you haven't joined the Diablo pack yourself?"

She glanced away. "No. I'm not really pack material."

Not pack material was an understatement. She'd gone rogue, faked her own death, and hadn't trusted any of us when she'd been in danger from her ex. It was no surprise she wouldn't want to be tied to a pack. But if she hadn't joined them, what had she been up to the past six weeks? "Where have you been, Trish?"

She pressed her lips together into a flat line and shook her head.

It was my turn to let out a long sigh. "Can you at least tell me if Jax is safe with them?"

"Yes, of course," she said immediately. "Listen, I don't really have anything to share about Jax other than out of all the Alphas I've met, Kai's the only one I trust."

"Okay." I wasn't sure what else to say. She obviously

wasn't going to give me anything on Jax, but I did appreciate her opinion on Kai. Even though I'd liked the Alpha, it was encouraging to know that wasn't just a good first impression.

Trish finally came and sat gingerly in the chair next to me. She bit down on her lower lip and then asked, "Have you seen Ty?"

"Today?"

"Today, yesterday... Any time this week?" Trish picked at her cuticles, clearly nervous.

"Sure," I said with a nod. "I saw him yesterday. He and Kennedy stopped by for dinner."

Her voice was halting when she asked, "How is he?"

"He's... okay. Adjusting." I wasn't sure what I could tell her. Ty wasn't communicating much with his mother. He'd wanted space to sort through his jumbled emotions. But she was calling all the time, and now she'd just shown up out of the blue. I was certain that she hadn't bothered to ask him if it was okay to stop by. Needless to say, her persistence wasn't going to go over well. "He just needs time, Trish. He'll come around when he's ready."

She lifted her head and narrowed her eyes at me. "You're not encouraging him to ignore me, are you?"

Blood surged through my veins, and I wanted nothing more than to lash out at her. But I held back my snarky comments and tried for calm. "Of course not, Trish. Ty is his own man. He doesn't need me telling him how to feel. But I do have to say it hurts a little that you think I'd do that. I'm not here to come between you and Ty."

"You're not?" she challenged.

I ground my teeth together. "No. I'm not." I turned my

attention to the melting ice cream, and with a sigh, I got up to put it back in the freezer. My dinner would have to wait.

"It sure seems like—" Trish started but cut herself off when the door opened.

"Marion?" Ty called. "I'm going out, do you need anything?"

"More ice cream. Mine melted." I walked back into the living room and spotted Ty staring at his mother, anger flashing like lightning in his dark eyes.

"What are you doing here?" Ty asked, his voice tight.

Trish stood and turned to face her son. "I came to talk to my son. You can't keep ignoring me forever."

"No? *You* did. You left me for five years and then suddenly you're here, trying to be a part of my life again? That's not how it works." Ty grabbed the door handle and started to walk back out.

"Where are you going?" she asked.

He paused. "I have plans."

"Are you going to meet Carson?"

I sucked in a sharp breath, knowing this was a sore subject for Ty. Carson was his older brother Trish had hid from him his entire life. In addition to Trish faking her own death, she'd kept Carson's entire existence a secret from Ty. It was no wonder Ty didn't trust his mother.

His voice was low and full of warning when he said, "That's none of your business."

I watched as Ty stalked out and then turned my attention to Trish. "I told you he just needs some time. Pushing isn't going to help."

She turned on me. "You don't need to tell me about *my*

26

son. I'm the one who raised him for eighteen years. Not you. I know what he needs."

"You think so?" There was a time when I'd have agreed with her. But not anymore. Ty had been through so much since Trish had disappeared. And after the pain he'd suffered when she faked her death, she couldn't just expect him to welcome her back into his life with open arms. He might be a grown man, but he was also still just a kid trying to come to terms with the fact that his mother abandoned him, and the last thing he needed was her pushing him to do anything he wasn't ready to do.

"I know so." The venom in her tone made me take a long look at her. And what I saw was a woman with deep regret.

The door swung open again, and we both turned to find Kennedy, Ty's boyfriend, standing just inside the entrance. "What happened with Ty?"

I tilted my head toward Trish.

Kennedy's gaze landed on her, and realization flashed in his eyes. "Oh. I guess that explains it."

"Explains what?" Trish demanded.

"Why Ty took an inch of rubber off his tires trying to get the hell out of here," Kennedy explained. He glanced at me. "I'm taking Paris Francine on a walk. Do you want me to take Minx, too?"

I eyed the pup crashed out on the couch and shook my head. "I think she's tucked in for the night, but thanks for asking. I'm sure Charlotte appreciates it."

"Kennedy," Trish called out. "I need you to do something for me."

He frowned. "You need *me* to do something for *you*?"

"I need my son to talk to me. So I need you to talk some sense into him. Do you understand?"

"Trish—" I started.

She whirled on me. "I wasn't talking to you, Marion. Butt out." She scowled at me and then hurried to Kennedy. "Please, I'm begging for your help here. I know Ty will listen to you."

Kennedy glanced at me and then cleared his throat. "I'm sorry, Ms. Kirkwood, but I'm not comfortable getting in the middle of things between you and Ty. I think you're just going to have to wait until he's ready."

"You little—" she snarled.

"Hey, jackass! Step away from the kid," Celia demanded as she popped in out of nowhere. The ghost was standing with her hands on her hips, glaring at Trish.

"And if I don't?" Trish challenged.

"Oh, this is going to be good," I muttered as I walked over to Kennedy and put an arm around him.

Celia cocked her head to the side and raised a mocking eyebrow. "I'll haunt you every day from now until forever. Imagine me stalking you while you're in the shower, on a date, having a little personal time." She gave Trish a sinister smile. "Wouldn't that be fun?"

"You think so?" Trish asked, appearing unconvinced. "I think a little sage would send you back to wherever you came from."

Celia threw her head back and laughed. "You could try, but I'd just show up again. Hopefully right about the time you get some hunky man naked. I could be the peanut gallery."

I couldn't help the laugh that escaped my lips.

Trish glared at me and then stalked out without saying another word.

"I guess that takes care of her," Celia said with an exaggerated hair flip.

"Thanks, Celia," Kennedy said, giving her a small smile.

"No thanks necessary, cutie," she quipped. "That was fun." She winked and then vanished again.

Kennedy shook his head slightly. "You know, it used to unsettle me when she'd just show up, but she's really grown on me."

I laughed. "Me, too, Kennedy. Me, too."

CHAPTER 4

The silence in my house was unnerving. It never used to be. I'd lived alone for years and if I was honest, I'd relished the silence. But then not long after I'd moved to Premonition Pointe, my sister Charlotte had shown up and she and Minx had moved in. Silence wasn't in either of their natures.

I glanced at the foot of my bed and spotted the little Chihuahua curled up, sleeping soundly. She really was cute in her sweet little daisy-print dress. And I had to admit that once she'd gotten used to me and her new home, she'd calmed down quite a bit.

Of course, I was half convinced that she was just depressed since her favorite person in the whole world hadn't been around for six weeks. I let out a long sigh and then snuggled down into my covers.

Just as my eyes were drifting closed, Minx suddenly jumped up and started barking at the top of her lungs.

"Minx! What the heck is it?" I shot out of bed and Minx

followed suit, jumping to the floor and sprinting toward the closed door. "Did your mama come home tonight?" I asked her as I opened the door.

The little dog darted out and ran full speed toward the living room. I grabbed my robe and wrapped it around myself as I followed her. "Char?" I called. "What happened? I thought you were staying with Denver."

"It's not Char," a raspy, familiar voice said.

I froze, afraid I was dreaming.

"Marion?" Jax asked softly. "Is it okay that I'm here?"

I blinked rapidly as my eyes finally adjusted to the darkness. The man I'd ached for night after night stood in front of me, holding Minx as she excitedly covered his cheek with doggie kisses. Her little tail was wagging so fast it was just a blur in the semi-darkness. "Jax?" I finally forced out, my voice cracking.

"Surprise." He flashed me a wry smile. "I would have called, but once I decided I needed to see you, I just jumped in my truck and headed straight here."

I let out a rush of air I hadn't even realized I was holding and cried with delight as I ran to wrap my arms around him. "You're here," I said into his neck. "I can't believe it."

He circled one strong arm around my waist and pulled me in until I was molded against the right side of his body. We stood there like that for a long moment, Jax and I practically fused together in a tight hug with Jax still holding Minx.

"How long are you staying?" I finally asked.

Jax released me, and after giving Minx a kiss on her head, he gently placed her on the couch. He took me by the hand and led me through my bedroom and into my en suite bathroom. Without saying a word, he turned the water on in the shower. He took a step back and without turning around, he placed one hand on the glass, bent his head, and ran a hand through his hair.

Exhaustion rolled off him in waves, and I couldn't shake the overwhelming feeling that he was near a breaking point. Silently, I stepped up behind him, circled my arms around him and went to work slowly unbuttoning his flannel shirt.

Jax lifted his head and placed both of his hands on my forearms as his thumbs gently caressed my skin as I worked. Once his shirt was unbuttoned, I tugged it off and then circled him until I stood in front of him and went to work on his jeans. Jax let me completely undress him and then watched with smoky eyes as I tugged my pajamas off. When I was finally bare, he sucked in a sharp breath and whispered, "God, I've missed you."

Tugging him into the shower, I let out a contented sigh and said, "Tell me I'm not dreaming."

His lips twitched into a hint of a smile. "You're not dreaming."

"Is that a promise?"

He gently pushed me into the spray and then dipped his head, claiming my lips for his own. His kiss was slow yet demanding. The kind of kiss that was intended to remind me who I belonged to. Jax buried his hands in my hair, tilting my head to one side to kiss me deeper.

Everything about him was passion and need with a hint of desperation. The past six weeks melted away, and I reveled in being consumed by this man I loved with my entire soul. Jax trailed one hand down the back of my neck, his rough fingers gentle as he pulled away, short of breath.

He pressed his forehead to mine and his hard body started to tremble.

"Are you cold?" I asked, turning him so that his body was under the warm spray.

But Jax just shook his head, running both hands over my skin as if he wasn't quite sure I was real.

I got the distinct impression that he needed something more from me other than just sex. There was no doubt he had every intention of making love to me, but right now, he needed *me*. Needed to be taken care of. Shown that he was missed and not a lost soul to the wolf curse. I had every intention of showing him that he was important. That he belonged right here with me, wolf curse or no. None of that mattered to me. I pressed my hand to his chest just over his heart and said, "I love you, Jax Williams."

Gooseflesh popped out over his skin despite the hot water sluicing over him.

"Let me take care of you," I whispered as I pumped some shampoo into the palm of my hand.

Jax didn't say anything. He just closed his eyes and leaned into me, pressing soft kisses to my collar bone.

I wrapped my arms around him and brought my hands up, massaging his scalp as I washed his hair.

Letting out the smallest groan of pleasure, Jax rested his forehead on my shoulder as I poured every ounce of my love into washing his worries away. I took my time reacquainting myself with his body, running my hands over his shoulders and gently kneading the tension I found there.

Jax reached up and covered one of my hands with his own and then brought my palm to his lips, kissing me softly. A shiver skittered over my skin, and all I wanted in that moment was to be held by the man I'd been missing for weeks.

As if Jax could read my mind, he turned and tugged me into his arms, burying one hand in my hair and pressing one to the small of my back as he molded me to him and claimed my lips with a passion so fierce it took my breath away.

This was what I'd been missing. The connection we'd shared had always been intense, but this was something else. Something more. A coming together of two souls. I hadn't felt right since the day Jax had left town. Suddenly I felt whole again and as if my world had righted itself.

"I need you, Marion," Jax whispered as he trailed kisses down my neck.

"I'm yours," I answered, digging my nails into his back.

Jax let out a low growl before turning me so that I was facing the wall. His hands cupped my heavy breasts and then one slid between my legs, making my eyes roll to the back of my head as pleasure rippled from my center all the way to my fingertips.

"You're always ready for me," he said, his finger stroking me.

"I was ready the moment I stepped into this shower." Placing my hands against the shower tile, I braced myself and glanced back at him. "Now, Jax."

His lips twitched into a sexy half smile as he grabbed my hips and yanked me against him, his erection pressed against my backside. I ground against him, desperate for him to take me.

He thrust against me once and then pulled back. In the

next moment, he was sliding into me, pulling a desperate moan from my lips.

"Never again, Marion," he said as he buried himself inside of me. "From this day forward, I'm going to start and end each day with you beside me. Understand?"

"Yes," I said with a nod. "Every morning and every night."

"That's right. You're mine." He pulled out and slammed back in as his hands clutched my breasts.

"Yours," I repeated, covering one of his hands and guiding his fingers to lightly pinch one of my nipples.

He chuckled softly. "Don't be so impatient, love. I was getting to that."

"I. Can't. Wait," I panted.

And then his hands were everywhere. My mind was blown with sensation as I got completely lost in Jax. He claimed me, made every inch of my body his. And when we both finally cried out from pleasure, my whole body went limp. If it hadn't been for Jax's strong arms holding me up, I'd have crumpled right there in the shower.

"Damn, I missed that," Jax breathed.

I let out a small chuckle and said, "Welcome home."

CHAPTER 5

I snuggled in the bed next to Jax, tracing my fingers over a series of red marks on his shoulder. "What happened here?"

"Just some scratches from being in the woods," he said without looking back at me.

The mental image of him racing around the woods in wolf form flashed in my mind and made my stomach ache with nervous energy. While we'd been in the shower, he'd said he was going to fall asleep and wake up next to me every morning and night, but had that just been hyperbole? Something he wanted, but couldn't really do? I was too afraid to ask. Right in that moment, I just wanted to believe that he was back for good. That we'd go back to our lives the way they'd been before he'd taken off to explore what it meant for him to be a wolf.

Jax let out a contented sigh and explained. "We were clearing a walking path in the woods behind the winery when a limb fell and grazed me."

"So you weren't chasing an elk through the woods in wolf form?"

He let out a bark of laughter. "No. I never was much of a hunter. My new status hasn't changed that. Though I did chase off a coyote one night."

The unease in my gut started to dissipate. "So no venison for you?"

"Nope."

"That's good to hear." I continued to trace his muscles, delighting when gooseflesh popped out over his skin. "Do you want to talk about why you're here and not with the pack?"

Jax was silent for so long, I was convinced that he wasn't going to answer me at all. But then he rolled over and cupped my cheek with his palm. "In the beginning, when I went out there, I needed to learn what it meant to be a wolf."

When he didn't elaborate, I asked, "Did you find out?"

"Yes." He glanced away, staring off into the darkness. When he finally met my gaze again, he said, "All of the other wolves in the pack were looking for family. Acceptance. A place to belong. It was as if the moment they were bitten, they found themselves feeling out of place in the lives they'd built before the bite. For a while, I thought that was to be my fate, too. As a wolf, I felt… different."

"Different how?" My heart was beating rapidly, and I was terrified that this might end up being a goodbye instead of the homecoming I thought it was.

"Like I no longer knew who I was. I suppose I was trying to figure that out."

I placed my hand over his and squeezed. "Did you?"

He let out a humorless chuckle. "Yeah. I figured out that I felt different because I *am* different. I eat more, sleep less, and feel claustrophobic if I spend too much time indoors. You know what's *not* different?"

"What?"

"My desire to be here. To be working with my hands, building things. I don't feel the need to belong to a pack. I'm not looking to find a new family. Mine is right here... with you."

My lips twitched into a pleased smile. "So this means you're here for good?"

He nodded. "If that's okay with you."

"More than okay." I leaned in and kissed him softly. "I might never let you leave again now that I have you back."

He laughed softly. "Are you going to chain me in the basement?"

"Only on the full moon," I said with a wink.

His chuckle turned into full laughter. "I'd be concerned if you actually had a basement."

I laughed along with him, and when we finally sobered, he said, "Seriously though. I will likely meet up with the pack once a month or so for a run when I need to shift. But otherwise, I'm not at all interested in being a regular member of the pack. My place is here."

"I can work with that." I cuddled in close, and when Jax wrapped his arms around me, I felt whole for the first time in weeks.

I WOKE to the delicious scent of coffee and chocolate.

"Morning, Sunshine," Jax said, holding my favorite mug out to me.

"You're a god," I said, pushing myself up and taking the coffee mug. After one sip, I let out a moan of pleasure. "I think I could get used to this."

"So could I," he said, his gaze traveling down to my breasts that were barely covered with the quilt.

I smirked. "That's the other way I like to be woken up."

"I know. And if I hadn't woken up at dawn, I might just have taken that route, but instead, I decided to let you sleep while I went out for these." He produced an open pastry box that was full of chocolate croissants.

"You went out already?" I asked, shocked. "I didn't even hear you leave."

"You were pretty out of it." He kissed me on the forehead. "The fog is already burning off. When you're done there, would you mind taking a walk with me down on the beach?"

It was something we'd done regularly before he'd taken off to figure out how to be a wolf. The fact that he wanted to fall right back into old habits made me grin. "Absolutely. Give me about ten minutes, and I'll be ready to go."

"Take your time. I'll be in the living room giving Minx the attention she deserves."

At the sound of her name, the little dog came running into the room and started barking madly at Jax.

"Cool your jets, little one," he said softly. "I'm coming."

Minx immediately stopped barking and stared up at him with adoration.

"I feel exactly the same way, Minx," I told her. "Enjoy

him while you can because as soon as I'm dressed and ready, he's all mine again."

Minx let out a little growl.

Jax shook his head as he scooped her up. "None of that, now," he said to the dog. "Let's go get you a treat while your aunt Marion finishes her coffee."

The dog snuggled into his chest, and all I could do was shake my head in amusement. Jax really had been missed, and although neither Minx nor I were wolves, we definitely considered him part of our pack.

CHAPTER 6

*T*wenty-five minutes later, Jax and I had left Minx behind and were walking along the shoreline. It was a gorgeous late October morning with plenty of sun shimmering off the deep blue of the ocean. There was still a bit of fog clinging to the tops of the rock outcroppings, and it was the type of morning that made me wish time would stand still.

"I missed this," I said as I leaned into Jax.

He placed his arm around my shoulders. "So did I."

The sound of the waves crashing against the shore was music to my ears. Had I come out here at all since Jax had left? Only once, maybe twice, and that had been something I'd done regularly even before Jax and I had gotten together. But without him, it had just made me too sad. I'd taken to walking around the neighborhood instead of the beach, which was one of the reasons I'd moved to Premonition Pointe almost a year ago. I'd forgotten just how much I loved feeling the sand between my toes.

"Jax? Marion?" a man called from behind us.

We both turned and to my surprise, Kai Gray was heading straight for us.

"Kai," Jax said, his brows pinched. "What are you doing out here? You weren't looking for me, were you?"

"No, no. Nothing like that," Kai said with an easy smile. "I was just out for a morning run when I spotted you both. Thought I'd say hi." He reached out and squeezed my hand briefly. "It's good to see you again, Marion."

Jax looked between us. "You know each other?"

"We met yesterday," I said, raising a hand in greeting at the Alpha.

"You've got a good woman here, Jax. I can see why you've had a hard time deciding whether you should be part of the pack," Kai said.

Jax grimaced. "About that. I won't be coming back." He pulled me in closer, tightening his arm around me. "My place is here with Marion."

Kai gave him a knowing nod. "I already knew that. I was just waiting for *you* to figure it out. You definitely aren't cut out for pack life. You're one of the independent ones."

"Yeah, well, I'm back where I belong," Jax said pulling me in closer as he tightened his hold on me even more.

"I can see that," Kai said, eyeing me. When he shifted his gaze back to Jax, he added, "You're welcome at the winery any time. I hope you know that."

"Thanks," Jax said. "I appreciate that."

It was strange watching the two men. They were being pleasant and polite with each other, but I got the impression there was something unsaid going on between them. I just couldn't put my finger on it.

"Listen, Jax," Kai said. "I'm going to go ahead with those plans to build a barn. I'd really like to hire you and your crew if you have time."

"Sure, man. Let me talk to my foreman and figure out what's on the schedule. I'll call you later today and we'll work it out."

When Jax had taken off to figure out how to live with being a wolf, he'd left his right-hand man in charge, and I'd been checking in periodically just to make sure everything was going okay. Luckily, Jax didn't have anything to worry about. While there'd been a few hang-ups, for the most part, his business was still thriving.

"Perfect," Kai said. "That'd make my life a lot easier."

The two men shook hands, and then Kai pulled Jax in for a quick bro hug.

"Help! Help!" a young voice called, sounding frantic.

I turned and my breath caught when I spotted a little boy running into the ocean, chasing after his dog that seemed to be swept up in the surf. "No!" I forced out, breaking into a sprint toward the kid.

But before I could get to the water, both Kai and Jax sprinted past me. Jax reached the boy first and plucked him out of the water while the boy continued to scream for his dog. Kai dove into the water, disappearing under the waves, and when he reappeared, he popped up right next to the dog. In mere moments, Kai had the black dog in his arms and was walking out of the surf.

"Thank you, thank you, thank you!" a woman cried as she ran toward the boy, who couldn't have been more than nine years old.

Jax was crouched down, talking to the boy as he pointed

at the woman who must have been his mother. But the boy shook his head, and instead of running to his mother, he darted over to Kai and fell to his knees as the dog ran into his arms.

"Cody!" The woman cried, sounding exasperated. "I told you to keep him on his leash."

The boy buried his head into the dog's neck and held on tightly as his mother shook her head.

I hurried over to Jax, reaching him at the same time as the mom.

The woman threw herself at Jax, wrapping her arms around him and squeezing him tightly. "You saved my boy," she cried. "I owe you my life."

Jax gently removed her from his body. "You don't owe me anything, ma'am. I just did what anyone would do."

"No. You're a hero." She grabbed him again and pressed a kiss to his cheek.

"Lacey! What the hell are you doing?" a man wearing a pair of ripped jeans and a white tank top barked at her.

"This man saved my son," she said, leaning against Jax and patting his chest.

There wasn't anything flirty about the woman's demeanor. It was clear she was just grateful and relieved, but the man grabbed her wrist and yanked her away from Jax. "You're making a fool of yourself, Lace. Throwing yourself at that man."

Lacey pushed at his chest with her free hand as angry fire blazed from her gaze. "I'm not, but even if I was, it's no business of yours. You made sure of that when you fucked my neighbor. Now go away. I already told you it was over. Find someone else to deal with your excessive drinking and inability to remain faithful for even two weeks."

"I already told you that was a mistake," he growled and tightened his hold on her wrist, making her wince.

"Hey," I said. "Let go of her wrist. You're hurting her."

"Stay out of it, Grandma," he growled.

"Grandma?" I parroted, offended. While I was certainly old enough to be a grandmother, I had never had anyone imply I looked like one. "That was uncalled for."

"Listen, buddy," Jax said evenly. "Why don't you just calm down? There's nothing to be upset about here."

"Mind your own fucking business." The man pushed Lacey in front of him, making her fall to her knees, and then he roughly pulled her back up by her forearm.

"Stop, John! That hurts," she cried as she tried to get to her feet but stumbled again.

"Mom!" the boy, Cody, called as he and the dog ran over to them. He stood in front of his mother, his face defiant as he glared at John. "Don't touch her."

I saw it coming, knew the man was about to strike the boy, and tried to lunge forward, intending to put myself between them. But Jax wrapped his arm around my middle, holding me back. "Let go!" I ordered but then fell silent as I watched Kai kick out and sweep the man off his feet.

John hit the beach with a thud, his face turning almost purple as pure rage radiated off him. He jumped back up and got in Kai's face. "You dumb son of a bitch. You're gonna pay for that."

Keeping his arm around me, Jax moved us so that we stood in front of Lacey and the boy, effectively shielding them from the altercation between Kai and John.

"We'll see about that," Kai said calmly and then ducked as John took a swing at him. The other man, outraged, went at Kai with both fists flying. With a deadly serious calm, Kai dodged each of his blows with precision. And then on John's last swipe, Kai tripped him again, sending the man face-first into the sand. Kai placed one foot on the man's back and pressed down right between his shoulder blades.

The other man forced out, "Can't. Breathe."

"That's too bad, isn't it? I'll tell you what. I'll let you up and let you walk away under your own steam if you commit to leaving this woman and her child alone." Kai lessened the pressure on the man's back just long enough for him to respond.

"And what if I don't?"

"Then this fight we're having is going to go very differently. And it won't be in your favor," Kai said coldly.

There wasn't any reason not to believe Kai. He'd handled John so perfectly, and it was easy to imagine a scenario where John got his ass handed to him so hard he'd likely need medical attention.

When John didn't respond, Kai increased the pressure on his back again.

John let out a groan, and in a halting voice, he said, "Fine. You win."

"I don't want to win," Kai practically growled. "I want you to keep your hands off this woman and her child. And while you're at it, don't ever bother them again. Got it?"

John's face had turned so red it was starting to look purple. Finally he nodded and gasped out, "Got. It."

Kai released the man, stepped back, and crossed his arms over his chest. "Good. You can go now."

Growling, John stood up and got right in Kai's face. His hands were clenched into fists, but he made no move to attack Kai again. "You can threaten me all you want, but in the end, you'll be the one wishing you'd never stepped foot in this town."

"We'll see," Kai said with a shrug, looking unbothered.

"Is there a problem here?" a voice called from behind us.

I spun and spotted two of Premonition Pointe's finest quickly making their way toward us, and I wondered who'd called them. My gaze drifted to Lacey, who'd moved away from us and was halfway up the beach. Cody was standing in front of her while she clutched his shoulder with one hand, and the other held the phone to her ear.

That explained it. I couldn't help but think this wasn't the first time Lacey had called the cops on her ex. The realization made me furious for her. No woman should ever have to endure such harassment.

"Everything's fine, officer," John said through clenched teeth. "Just a little misunderstanding."

The two cops glanced at each other and then eyed John and Kai. "We've had a complaint about harassment, Mr. Vincent. Want to explain why you broke the terms of your restraining order?"

"I didn't!" John insisted. "I was out for walk when I happened upon Cody and Lacey. This is public property, miles away from their house. How was I supposed to know they were here?"

"Ms. Riley says you laid hands on her. Are you saying that isn't true?" the cop asked.

John clamped his mouth shut and narrowed his eyes in Lacey's direction.

The cop let out a sigh and pulled out his cuffs. "I'm sorry, Mr. Vincent, but you're under arrest for violating the restraining order." He began to read the man his rights and then hauled him back up the beach.

"I'll need your statements," the remaining officer said to us.

"Of course, Officer"—I peered at his badge—"Stone." I answered his questions, explaining what I'd seen.

When Stone was satisfied, he turned to Jax and Kai. His demeanor instantly turned hostile. "Do you have anything to add to Ms. Matched's statement?"

Both Kai and Jax shook their heads.

"I figured that was the case." Stone sneered at Kai and added, "I don't know what made your kind move to Premonition Pointe, but if I were you, I'd seriously think about moving on."

"Why?" I asked before either of the men could say anything.

"His kind aren't welcome here," Stone said, nodding to Kai.

I had the distinct impression that Officer Stone had no idea that Jax was also Kai's *kind*, but I certainly wasn't going to correct him. "That's not very neighborly of you, Officer Stone," I said coldly. "A less charitable person might even call it bigoted."

He scowled at me before turning his attention back to Kai. "We're watching you, *Alpha*." Then without another word, the officer took off after his partner.

"That was—" I started.

"To be expected," Kai said with a shrug. "It's not the first time the pack has received a less than friendly welcome to a town. I'm sure once they realize we aren't here to make trouble, they'll go back to pretending we don't exist."

"That's awfully charitable of you," I said, horrified by the way the officer had treated him. Just because he was a wolf didn't mean he was some sort of criminal. I made a mental note to mention the incident to Brix, the man Charlotte and I worked with at the Magical Task Force, just in case there was something more going on with the police department than just hateful bigotry.

"The alternative is to spend my entire life angry, and I'm just not willing to do that," Kai said.

I had to admire the man. If I were in his shoes, I probably would spend way too much time wishing boils on people who deserved it. And considering I was a witch, there was more than a zero percent chance that I could somehow make that happen without actually casting a spell. It had happened to Grace when she'd wished erectile dysfunction on her cheating ex. I had to hold back a chuckle as I remembered her telling me that story.

Jax clasped Kai on the shoulder and said, "I'll try to come by later this afternoon, and we can talk about that barn."

"Sounds good."

The pair engaged in another bro hug before Kai waved at me. "Talk to you soon, Marion."

"Absolutely," I called after him as he took off down the beach.

"That wasn't what I envisioned happening when I asked you to take a walk on the beach with me," Jax said.

I leaned into him and clasped my fingers around his.

"You were great, though, running into the water to help that boy."

"I did what anyone would do," he said with a shrug.

I knew better. While there certainly were people who would drop everything help someone in need, I'd also seen far too many other people who either didn't want to get involved or who ended up freezing when faced with a challenging situation. If there was a choice, Jax would always be the hero.

"Did I tell you how glad I am you're back?" I asked him.

Jax's lips twitched into a small smile before he leaned down and gave me a sweet kiss. "I'm glad I'm back, too."

"I'd give you a hug right now, but those wet clothes don't look very appealing. How about we go home and get you out of those?" I asked, letting my gaze roam up and down his body.

"You don't have to ask me twice." Jax grabbed my hand, and we took off toward the trail that led to the street parking.

Just as we emerged onto the sidewalk, I spotted Autumn standing by a black Mercedes and staring at a red truck that was parked halfway up the street. "Autumn?"

She startled and pressed a hand to her chest. "Goodness. I didn't see you there."

"That's because you were too busy staring at that sexy red truck."

"It's not the truck I was staring at," she said, her cheeks flushing pink. "It was the guy that got in it. Man, he's hot. In fact, I haven't stopped thinking about him since I met him in your office."

"Kai Gray?" I asked, amused.

"Yes." She fanned herself with her hand. "He's just so damned good-looking."

Jax cleared his throat, and I got the impression he was trying to cover a laugh.

I squeezed his hand and turned my attention back to Autumn. "You like Kai?"

"Well, I don't know him, really, but I like what I see." She glanced back up the hill in the direction where the red truck had disappeared.

"How do you feel about dating shifters?" I hedged. She'd mentioned yesterday that she didn't think she was ready to date someone who howled at the moon, but I was pretty sure that'd been a joke.

"Shifters?" she asked and slid her gaze to Jax. She'd learned he was a shifter when they'd met briefly at my office. It was obvious she approved of what she saw. "I hadn't really thought seriously about it before, but if you're thinking of setting me up with Kai, then yes. I'm in. You only live once, right?"

I laughed. "Yes, that's exactly what I was thinking. I'll be in touch with details soon, okay?"

"Sounds perfect." She grinned at me and then at Jax before she took off down the trail.

"What was that about?" Jax asked as we made our way up the hill toward my small house.

"I guess I haven't had a chance to tell you yet, but the reason I met Kai yesterday is because he came into the office. He hired me to find him a match. Someone he can be partners with who is outside of the pack dynamic."

"Really?" Jax seemed surprised, but then after a couple seconds, he nodded. "Yeah. That makes some sense."

"How?" I asked, curious about the alpha.

"I'd heard that Kai used to have a mate, but she went rogue when he wouldn't cave to her whims. Apparently, she had expensive tastes and got angry when Kai wouldn't commit to buying them a fancy place in Jackson Hole. According to the rumors, she really did him dirty after she realized he was never going to live the lifestyle she craved. In the end, she left him and the pack for another wolf who was known for running black market businesses, which led to money laundering and everything that goes along with living that sort of life. It caused a lot of problems with Kai's pack when she opened up credit lines using the pack's LLC information and maxed them out, leaving the pack with an outrageous amount of debt. It took Kai a couple of years to clear the credit reports."

"That's awful," I said, devastated for Kai. How could someone who supposedly loved you do something like that?

"It was. Ever since then, Kai hasn't really dated. At least according to the pack members I talked to. I don't blame him for wanting to date outside of the pack. After all that, I'd want to date someone who clearly was there for me, not just the power that comes with being part of team Alpha."

"Same. Luckily, he won't have to worry about that with Autumn. She's a laid back, self-made woman who isn't looking for anyone to take care of her. She wants a partner, not a sugar daddy."

Jax stared at me. "Sugar daddy?"

"You know, a man who lavishes gifts and money on a

woman with the expectation that she show him some affection."

"I know what it is," Jax said with a laugh. "I just didn't think the term applied to fifty-something-year-old-women."

I cracked up at that, knowing he had a point. But I still lightly swatted his arm. "Don't be ageist."

"Yes, ma'am." He mimed tipping his hat at me. In the next moment he sobered. "Seriously though, I hope Autumn works out for him. Or someone equally as grounded. Kai deserves a partner who can be his support system. Because right now, he's the backbone of that pack. Without him, they'd be an unruly bunch."

"Really?"

Jax nodded. "Kai keeps them in line. If he dates someone outside of the pack, he won't have to worry about the power dynamics. It's a solid plan. I hope it works out for him."

"From your lips to the goddess's ears," I said. "I have a lot riding on this, too. Autumn is my marketing plan to get my business back on its feet. If they don't work out, that's going to blow up in my face."

"Are you sure they'd be a good fit?" Jax asked.

"I'm not just sure, I know. Their auras are a perfect match," I said.

"Then you have nothing to worry about. When was the last time your aura-reading ability was off?"

"Ha! About thirty years ago when I decided *we* weren't compatible," I said with a hollow laugh. "Remember that?"

He gave me a sympathetic frown. "I remember all too well. But I think things turned out the way they were supposed to. If we'd stayed together back then, I think the chances of us crashing and burning were high. But now? Now I know exactly who and what I want, and nothing's going to take me away from you again."

"Promise?" I demanded.

He paused and kissed me softly before whispering, "Promise."

CHAPTER 7

"Mind if I catch a ride with you out to the winery?" I asked Jax as I climbed out of bed and pulled on my robe. The minute we'd gotten back to my house, I'd followed Jax into the shower, and then we'd spend the next hour in bed, exploring each other's bodies until we were both sufficiently satisfied.

"We're going to need to shower again," he said with a smirk. "Those wolves will scent us the moment we step on the property."

I groaned. They'd immediately know what we'd been up to. "Fine. But we'll take turns this time. I have no confidence that we'll be able to keep our hands off each other for even ten minutes."

"You're no fun," he said with a smile as he lay back on the pillow with his hands behind his head.

I paused and let my gaze roam over his well-defined chest and wondered if I was crazy. Who cared if we couldn't keep our hands to ourselves? We would be in the shower after all.

Jax let out a rumble of laughter. "Go, before I follow you in there and we never leave this house again."

While that didn't sound half bad, I did as he said, and when I slipped under the spray of the hot water, I decided that solo showers were highly overrated.

"JAX, MARION," Kai called as we jumped out of Jax's truck. "I didn't expect both of you this afternoon."

"Marion has matchmaking business to discuss with you," Jax said, placing his hand on the small of my back as we walked over to the alpha.

"You do? Did you get that mixer set up?" Kai asked.

"Nope. It's a date," I said. "But we can talk about that after you and Jax are done with your business. Do you mind if I just take a look around?" I gestured to the gorgeous vineyard behind me. "I promise to not steal any grapes."

He laughed. "That thought never would have crossed my mind. Sure, take a look around. We'll talk before you go."

Jax kissed the top of my head, and then the two men wandered off toward an old stable that had seen much better days.

I turned toward the grapes and couldn't help walking toward them. I'd always thought California vineyards in the fall were what heaven must look like. The golden hues of the leaves reminded me of a spectacular sunset that lasted for three months. I could have stood at the end of the row of grapes, transfixed forever. I might have, too, if a man's voice hadn't broken the spell.

"Can I help you, ma'am?" he asked in a Southern drawl that made me question my reality. We were still in Premonition Pointe, weren't we?

"Ma'am," I said, shaking my head as I took in the tall, lanky young man who couldn't have been a day over twenty-five. "When did I become a ma'am?"

"I told you to stop saying that, Evan," another man chastised as he appeared from behind Evan. The new arrival had sun-bleached blond hair, bright blue eyes, and a charming, easy-going smile. If there was a picture in the dictionary next to the phrase *surfer dude*, this guy would be there. "The women around here don't like that word."

The Southern boy frowned. "It's a term of respect. It's not meant to insult anyone."

"I know," I said quickly and held out my hand. "Hi, I'm Marion. I'm meeting with Kai a little later when he's done discussing barns with Jax. And you are?"

He took my hand and held on tightly as he said, "Evan Abernathy, from the Louisville, Kentucky, Abernathys. It's a pleasure to meet you, Marion."

The surfer let out a snort of laughter. "You know she's Jax's woman, right? Flirting with her will only get you roughed up."

"I'm not flirting," Evan insisted. "I'm just minding my manners like my grandmother used to say."

"It's fine," I said, chuckling. "I'm not offended." Sort of. While it hurt my ego to be thought of as a ma'am, I certainly understood that the young man was just being polite. I turned to the surfer dude. "And you are?"

"Ryder."

"Of course, you are." I shook my head. What could be more appropriate than that?

"Sorry?" he asked, looking confused. "Do we know each other?"

"No. I just… never mind. It's not important. How about you guys show me around the place?"

"Sure," Evan said. "Come on. We'll give you the tour."

I spent the next half hour following Evan and Ryder around the property. They showed me all the grapes they were growing, the bunkhouse where they stayed, the new stables where they boarded a number of horses, and then finally the old stables where Kai's office was and where they kept some of the farming supplies.

"Right now, all the grapes go out to a processer," Ryder explained. "But once the barn is built, Kai is going to start processing our grapes in house. Gray Wolf Wines."

"It's gorgeous," I said, opening my arms wide and indicating the entire property.

"It really is," said another man who looked like he might be Ryder's twin as he rushed up to us and play-tackled Ryder. The two of them went down in the dirt and started wrestling while three more men appeared from the fields and started taking bets on who would pin the other one first.

Their cheers were loud and raucous, and I found myself being pulled away from the excitement by Evan.

"They get a little single-minded when they're like this. Kai would kill me if I let you get caught in the middle."

I glanced over at the two men rolling around in the dirt and understood what Evan was saying. They were going full bore, looking as if they were ready to crush the other one while their packmates stood off to the side, cheering on their favorites. "Does this happen often? Random fights that come out of nowhere?"

"With those two?" Evan snorted. "Yeah. But they're like brothers, so what do you expect?"

"Like brothers? They aren't?" I asked, confused.

"They're second cousins. Don't worry, everyone always thinks they are twins," Evan explained.

A loud, piercing whistle permeated the air, and all the commotion stopped at once.

"Enough," Kai barked as he joined the crowd. "I thought we were checking irrigation lines today. Did you degenerates get that done?"

Ryder and his cousin both scrambled to get to their feet. The other men groaned as they realized their bets were void and the entertainment would have to wait for another time.

"We were just getting ready to check the last few acres, Kai," Ryder said, sounding professional, but looking like he'd just been dragged through the mud. There was dirt smudged across his forehead and cheek, and his torn, mud-caked shirt looked like it should go straight into the bin when he took it off.

"Yeah, you looked like it. Go. Get it done before we lose the light," Kai said.

All the men disappeared back into the vineyard fields, and suddenly it felt as if Jax, Kai, and I were the only three people left on the property.

"That's amazing," I said. "How they all just do what you say without complaint. I know a lot of parents who'd love to learn your secret ways. Maybe you should write a book."

Kai shook his head. "Packs are different from families in some ways. The pack bond with the Alpha is something others can't just emulate. The magic exists because of the pack dynamic."

"Makes sense," I said. "Too bad you can't package and sell that. You'd be a rich man."

"Some things are worth more than money," he said lightly, and when I looked at Jax, I had no choice but to agree.

The sound of an engine roared, and the three of us watched as a red Toyota Tacoma spit gravel out from under its tires as it sped down the driveway.

Kai had his arms crossed over his chest while he waited for the driver to show themselves.

When the door opened, a tiny woman who couldn't have been taller than five feet jumped out. She hurried past me and stalked right up to Kai, shaking her finger and nearly poking him in the chest as she barked, "Ever since you *wolves* moved in here, it's been nothing but trouble. I knew I should have taken out that loan to buy this place. It would have saved me a major headache even if I didn't know what to do with it."

Kai sighed. "What trouble have we caused today, Fiona? Is the music too loud again? They like to listen while they're working, but I'll get the boys to turn it down."

What music? I wanted to ask. I hadn't heard a note since I'd stepped out of Jax's truck.

"No. It's much worse. You people broke the water line, and now I have no water at my house. No baths, no cooking, no filling my ice trays. You need to fix this, Kai Gray. Do you hear me? Otherwise, I'm filing a complaint."

"With who?" I blurted and instantly wished I'd kept my mouth shut when both Kai and Jax glared at me.

"The city business commissioner," she said with a sniff. "Who else?"

Who else, indeed. Fiona wasn't playing around. Apparently she really hated her new neighbors. That must have been a character flaw on her part, because from everything I'd seen, I wouldn't only want to be neighbors with them; I'd want to *adopt* one or two of them.

"Fiona," Kai said patiently, "we're not digging lines today. We couldn't have broken your water line."

Fiona narrowed her eyes at him. "I'm not stupid, Kai Gray. I see your men out there working on the water lines. And then mine went out. You do the math."

"They're just hooking up irrigation lines. The *above ground* lines," Kai tried to explain, but Fiona was already climbing into her truck and had her middle finger up in the air, flipping him off.

"Fix it, Kai Gray. Or else—"

"Yeah, you'll call the city. I heard you the first time." He turned to Jax. "Want to help me track down a broken water line?"

"Sure, brother." Jax glanced at me. "Want to wait here?"

I shook my head. "I'm going where you go."

His eyes flashed with amusement as the three of us headed toward Jax's truck.

Ten minutes later, the three of us were standing over an obviously cut water pipe that was about twenty feet from Fiona's house. It wasn't anywhere near the Gray property line, but Fiona was still insisting that one of Kai's boys had to be responsible.

"Ma'am," I said, stealing Evan's word. "I think you might be overreacting a little bit. Why would they do that?"

"Because they're hooligans. Why else?" Fiona was standing on her front porch, wearing dusty jeans and a bright pink T-shirt, and she had her arms crossed over her chest and her bottom lip pushed out like a petulant child.

"It's not productive to accuse people when you don't have any proof," I said. "Do you have any video footage?"

"I know it was one of them," Fiona insisted. "Who else would do this?" She turned and stomped into her house, and the screen door slammed shut behind her.

An ex-lover? Ex best friend? The mail carrier? I thought. Surely anyone who had to deal with her on a regular basis was ready to do more than just cut a water pipe and then leave it out in the open to make it easy to find.

"How about we just get this fixed and then get back to our day," Jax said, already pulling his toolbox out of his truck.

Kai nodded, tapped something out on his phone, and then rolled up his sleeves, ready to join Jax to fix the pipe. They'd just gotten the water main turned off when the rest of the pack appeared from the woods, all of them standing back while they evaluated the situation. "This line has been cut in two places," Kai pointed out. "We'll need two crews to get this done as fast as possible."

"No problem, Kai," Ryder said with a mock salute. Ryder spoke to the other wolves, relaying the information. There were a few grumbles, and who could blame them? They had plenty of work to do back at the winery. Taking time out to replace pipe hadn't been on the agenda.

Still, they all pitched in and were well on their way to

replacing the pipe when Fiona appeared from the house, her phone in one hand and a beer in the other. "The police are on their way. If any of you have warrants out for your arrest, here's your two-minute warning."

"Why?" I asked her, outraged. "They didn't do anything, yet here they are helping you. And you called the police?"

"I needed to report the incident, didn't, I?" Fiona said with a haughty sniff. "What better time than when all the suspects are here?"

Before I could say anything else, she stomped back into her house and slammed the door again.

Furious at the woman, I walked over to Kai and Jax and explained the situation. Jax was just as outraged as I was, but again, Kai just shrugged, maintaining his cool.

"My team didn't do this," Kai said. "She can call whoever she wants, but the truth will come out. It always does." The Alpha went back to shoveling the mud out from around the leak.

I turned to Jax. "Then why does it feel like we're walking into a firing squad?"

"Because we are," he said gently and then searched my eyes when he added, "This is what it means to be a wolf, Marion. Are you sure you're up for marrying one?"

"Marrying?" I forced out.

Jax's face flushed as he looked away, and I got the distinct impression he hadn't meant to say the M-word. "Well, yeah. Someday," he muttered.

"Someday," I repeated with a nod, feeling my gut flutter with nerves. Marriage wasn't something I thought about often. Not at my age, but the fact that it was on Jax's mind, especially while he was knee deep in mud... Well, that certainly gave me something to consider, didn't it?

"Stop looking at me like that," he said, exasperation in his tone. "I wasn't proposing."

"I know," I said and then grinned like a fool until I heard the sirens coming.

CHAPTER 8

"*L*ook, Stone, it's these two again," the same officer who'd arrested John earlier that day said with a sneer.

"Should have known," Stone replied.

I ground my teeth together, trying to keep my snarky responses to myself. Kai and Jax were still working on the damned pipe, and here they were being harassed by the police. And for what, being good neighbors?

Kai wiped his hands on a towel from Jax's truck and walked over to the policemen. "What can we do for you this afternoon, gentleman?"

"We're here to follow up on a destruction of property claim by Ms. Fitzgerald. She says the neighbors intentionally cut her water line. You wouldn't know anything about that, would you?" Stone asked.

"Nothing other than we volunteered to come over here and fix it," Kai said patiently.

"To cover your tracks?" the other officer asked.

I peered at his name badge. *X. Wallis.* I hadn't recognized him earlier that morning and now that I knew his name, I was certain he was new to Premonition Pointe. Had he always been an asshole, or had Stone rubbed off on him? The two made my stomach turn, and I wondered how it was possible Jax and I had just been talking about marriage and now he and Kai were being questioned for vandalizing Fiona Fitzgerald's property. As if it made any sense at all that they'd cut her pipe and then rush over to fix it.

"There are no tracks to cover," Kai said. "I don't know who did it, but it wasn't me, or Jax, or anyone who lives on the Gray Wolf Winery compound."

"How can you be sure? Do you keep trackers on your dogs even when they're in human form?" Stone asked with a sneer.

"That was uncalled for," I said, my voice shaking with rage. How dare these jackasses come here and talk to Kai and Jax like that?

"It was just a question, Ms. Matched. There's no need to get your fur ruffled." The two policemen cackled at the uninspired joke.

I rolled my eyes and wondered if I could get Brix to do an in-depth background check on these two idiots. Surely they'd done something that could get them suspended from the department. It was the least they deserved.

It suddenly hit me that if I ever did marry Jax, this was something I was going to have to get used to. There was no reason to believe that the blatant discrimination Kai and the pack was experiencing wouldn't affect him, too. Affect us. Was that something I could handle?

Absolutely. One hundred percent, I could deal with it. I'd

be damned if I'd let some ignorant jackasses keep me from marrying Jax because of their short-sighted views. If it came down to it, I'd walk through fire for Jax. If I had to spend the rest of my life clapping back at people like Stone and Wallis, I'd do it. Happily. Because eff them.

After being separated from Jax for six weeks, it was clear that wasn't something I ever wanted to do again.

"There you are," Fiona called from her porch. "I was beginning to think I needed to call the local donut shop to get one of you out here."

Stone's self-satisfied grin vanished as he glared at the woman.

I almost laughed out loud. It was slightly comforting to know that Fiona was a bitch to everyone, not just Kai and Jax.

"How about you just tell us what happened?" Stone said, holding a small tablet and a pen.

"Well, Officer, this afternoon I noticed the wolves next door doing some plumbing work." She waved in the direction of Kai's property. "And then when I went to shower about an hour ago, the water didn't turn on. Upon further inspection, I found this." Fiona pointed at the cut pipe. "Someone had dug up my water line and cut it clean with some sort of saw in *two places*." She held up two fingers for emphasis. "And then they just left it like that. When I went over to the wolf habitat, I found the lot of them covered in dirt as they hooked up water lines."

"Okaaaay," Stone said, eyeing her. "And why do you think they cut your water line?"

"We didn't cut anyone's water line," Kai interjected.

"We'll see about that, Mr. Gray," Wallis said, his voice cold.

"Because they want my property and they think if they torture me, I'll sell out." She gave Kai a dirty look. "I'm never giving up this land. It belonged to my great-granddaddy. So if it's a battle you want, then it's a battle you'll get."

"Is that true, Mr. Gray? Did you try to buy this property?" Stone asked.

"I did inquire about it when I was purchasing the adjacent land," Kai said slowly as if trying to measure his words. "When Ms. Fitzgerald made it clear she wasn't in the market to sell, I thanked her for her time, and that was that. I'm certainly not trying to make her life unpleasant so she'll move on. If I was doing that, do you think I'd be over here fixing the line?"

I suppressed a grimace. While there was less than zero proof, the circumstantial evidence against the Diablo Wolf Pack was likely to add up quickly. And with a biased police force, that meant nothing but trouble for Kai and the pack.

"I see," Stone said, sharing a look with Wallis.

Kai was cool as a cucumber when he added, "You're welcome to review my security footage from today if you think that will help. It won't show who did this,"—he pointed at the pipe—"but it will likely give an alibi to each of my pack members. They've been working on my land all day. The footage will show that."

Stone looked skeptical, but he nodded. "Yes, that would be helpful. I assume we can get that now?"

"You can. Just let me text the office and let them know you're coming." Kai whipped out his phone, sent a message, and then gave the officers a nod. "They'll meet you there.

The office is in the old stables just past the house, first door on the right."

I couldn't believe Kai was being so cooperative. It was also equally impressive that he trusted his pack so implicitly. How could he be a hundred percent certain none of them had done this? Even as a prank. Considering how surly Fiona was, it wouldn't surprise me if one of them got fed up and cut her pipe just to annoy her.

"We'll do that," Stone said. He glanced at Fiona. "If you think of anything else, give us a call. Otherwise, we'll be in touch."

"I want restitution!" she called. As the police car rolled down her driveway, she looked at Kai and Jax. "How soon until I can get that shower?"

"We're almost done here," Kai said. "Twenty minutes, give or take."

She eyed him for a long minute and then turned around and went back into the house.

"Holy hell," I said. "Kai, how were you able to remain so calm? If I was ready to scratch some eyes out, you must have been ready to throw down."

A muscle in Kai's jaw ticked as he closed his eyes and sucked in a deep breath. When he opened them, he stared me in the eyes and said, "If the pack is going to make a home here, we have to be able to get along with our neighbors and the local law enforcement. Right now, the only thing I can do is prove we're not a threat. That we will help when something goes wrong. It's why I'm here fixing this goddamned pipe when I know for certain none of my crew did this."

"How do you know?" Jax asked him as he screwed on a new section of pipe.

"One, I trust them," he said with a wry smile. "But also, there are perimeter alarms on the winery property. If anyone crossed them in either direction, I'd have been notified."

So that was why he was so certain his wolves hadn't done this. I let out a small chuckle. "It's really going to disappoint Stone when he realizes you were right."

Kai grinned. "I'd pay good money to see that." But then he sobered and ran a hand through his dark hair as he eyed Fiona's house. "The question is, who actually did this and why?"

I stepped up beside the alpha. "It's not hard to imagine someone having a grudge against Fiona. She's not exactly the warmest woman I've ever met."

Jax snickered from behind us.

"That's true," Kai agreed. "I just can't shake the feeling that this is a setup."

"By who?" I asked.

"I have no idea." He turned back to Jax. "Are we ready to turn the water back on?"

Jax nodded.

After they confirmed the pipe was fixed with no leaks, Kai let Fiona know she was in business. The woman didn't even bother thanking him. She just gave him a quick nod and shut the door.

A few minutes later, we were back at the winery.

"Do you need us for anything else?" Jax asked Kai.

"No. Just get me the estimate on the barn when it's ready." Kai turned to me. "I know you came out here to talk business, but can that wait? I'm just not in the mood to think about mixers or coffee dates."

"Of course. I actually wanted to let you know that Autumn Winters has shown interest in getting to know you. But you can think about that and call me when you have some time, and we'll talk more about it then."

He raised one eyebrow. "Autumn Winters? I'm definitely interested. She doesn't mind that I'm a wolf?"

"She doesn't at all." I grinned, knowing this would be the easiest love match I'd made in years.

"That's… good." He glanced away, looking almost shy, and then said, "I'll call you and we'll figure it out."

"Sure thing." I gave him a quick hug. Jax shook his hand and said he'd be in touch.

As Jax and I climbed into his truck, I leaned back and let out a long sigh. As happy as I was to see where the connection between Kai and Autumn went, I couldn't shake the overwhelming irritation that clung to me after witnessing the Premonition Pointe police officers treat Kai and Jax like criminals just because they were shifters. It was so wrong it made me want to scream. "Man. I can't believe the bullshit you guys had to deal with today. I don't think I've ever wanted to deck someone more than I did today. If there hadn't been a risk of spending the night in jail, I'd have popped Stone in the nose a couple of times. Not that Wallis was any better. The absolute nerve of—"

"Marion," Jax said gently, placing his hand on my arm. "I know you're upset, but Kai has been through this before. He's handling it the best way he knows how."

"Of course he is. It's just that he shouldn't have to take all that BS just to survive in this town. If the pack had been anyone else, they'd have been welcomed with open arms. Especially when they are opening a winery. That venue is going to be a huge revenue earner for everyone. The events they could have there will be a boon to so many other businesses. The people of this town should be throwing him and the pack a welcome to Premonition Pointe party. They shouldn't be accusing Kai of cutting pipes and acting like if the pack even breathes wrong, they'll wish they'd never stepped foot here."

I leaned back against the seat and just breathed.

"That was quite the rant," Jax said, putting the truck into gear and heading back to the main road.

"It was, wasn't it?" I said, softening.

"Feel better?"

"Marginally," I said as Jax pulled out onto the two-lane highway and I stared at the gorgeous property we were leaving. "It's just not right. No one deserves to be treated that way."

"You're right." He reached over and grabbed my hand, lacing his fingers between mine. He pulled my hand up and gently kissed my knuckles. "Thank you."

"For what?"

He squeezed my hand. "For being you."

CHAPTER 9

"What's for dinner?" Charlotte asked as she swept into the kitchen. Her red curls were piled on her head in a messy but stylish bun, and there were tendrils framing her face.

"Why? Are you planning on a snack before you go out?" I asked, eyeing her slim pencil skirt and lowcut, black wraparound blouse.

"I'm not going out." She went over to the small wine rack I'd installed on the wall and chose one of my favorite reds. "Will this go with what's cooking, or do I need to consider a white?"

I glanced down at the pan of manicotti I was building and said, "The red is perfect. Does this mean you're joining us?" Ty and Kennedy were coming for dinner, so I'd made enough for a small army. One never knew how much food a young twenty-something could put away.

"Denver and I are trying to save up for a tropical

vacation this winter, so we're pinching pennies. If it's okay with you, we'd love to join you guys."

It was on the tip of my tongue to make a snarky remark about who actually bought all the food and wine she'd be indulging in, but I swallowed it. My relationship with my younger half sister was better than it had ever been. And I didn't want to mess that up by being petty. "Sure, we'd love to have you join us. Just add two more place settings on the table."

"I'm on it." Charlotte beamed at me, and I had to take a second to appreciate the moment. My sister and I hadn't always gotten along. In fact, when she showed up on my doorstep just a few months after I'd moved to Premonition Pointe, I'd reluctantly agreed to letting her stay. She'd been spoiled and petulant while I'd been resentful. But somehow, after all these months, we'd finally worked past most of our issues. And for the first time in my life, I had a healthy relationship with my sister. Whoever said you can't teach an old dog new tricks had no idea what they were talking about. Because this perimenopausal woman had indeed learned to get over the past, and now I loved that my sister lived with me. Though, I wouldn't mind if she kicked in a little more for groceries every now and then.

"Wine now?" Charlotte asked, holding up the bottle.

"Yes, please," I said as I put the finishing touches on the manicotti. After I put the dish into the oven, I took a long swig of the wine and gave my sister a grateful smile. "I don't know why I didn't open that an hour ago."

She chuckled. "Thank the goddess you didn't, otherwise who knows what you would've put in the oven? You're not exactly known for holding your own when you're drinking wine."

"You've got a point," I conceded. "Vodka? I can drink that all night and still function just fine. But get more than two glasses of wine in me, and suddenly I need a keeper."

"Good thing I'm here then," Jax said as he walked up behind me and circled my waist with his arms.

"Hey, when did you get here?" I asked, turning and giving him a quick kiss. It was Sunday, and he'd taken his foreman out to lunch before they spent the afternoon going over the schedule and the books for his business.

"Just now. Dinner smells delicious," he said as he nodded hello to Charlotte.

"Wine?" she asked him.

"Absolutely." He grabbed a glass and handed it to her. While she was pouring, he washed his hands and then said, "Put me to work."

I handed him the French bread, the garlic butter, and a knife. "How was your meeting?"

"Good. We cleared some time to get Kai's barn built, so Sawyer and I went over there to check it out. We're sending a crew next week to get started."

"That's fantastic. Did Kai say if they'd had any more trouble with Fiona or the water line investigation?"

"No more trouble," Jax confirmed. "Though Kai did say that they never got back to him about the camera footage. He called and they finally, *reluctantly* admitted that it appeared no one from the winery had anything to do with Fiona's water line."

"Do they know who did?" I asked, leaning against the counter.

"Nope. Apparently Fiona has security cameras, too, but she wouldn't give them access. She said something about maintaining her privacy and that she wasn't going to be subjected to surveillance."

"Seriously?" Charlotte asked, her expression incredulous. "She's the one who wanted an investigation, right?"

I'd filled my sister in on what had gone down at Fiona's a few days ago. She was just as outraged as I'd been. And I loved her for it.

"Yes," Jax said with a humorless chuckle. "But since she won't cooperate, they've stopped looking into it."

I rolled my eyes. "Fiona is her own worst enemy."

"It sure seems like it," Jax agreed.

"Hello!" Ty called from the living room, followed by the unmistakable bark of their Yorkie, Paris Francine. Minx answered with a bark of her own, and the two dogs could be heard running through the house, no doubt chasing each other.

I poked my head out of the kitchen and spotted Ty, Kennedy, and Denver all trudging into the house. "Welcome. Charlotte will get you drinks while I finish up dinner."

"No rush," Kennedy said as he walked over and gave me a kiss on the cheek.

I smiled at Ty's boyfriend and once again found myself feeling grateful that he and Ty had found each other.

Denver leaned in and gave me a hug before he greeted Charlotte with a kiss.

I stood there, watching as most of the people I loved gathered around my table. My father Memphis and my aunt

Lucy hadn't been able to make it. They, along with their partners, had signed up for some card game tournament at a beachside bar, Hallucinations, in downtown Premonition Pointe. The ones who had made it were happily chatting and laughing and filling the house with joy. My gaze met Jax's, and I knew in that moment that life had never been more perfect.

Dinner was filled with good conversation, lots of laughs, and too much wine. I was just getting up to serve the tiramisu I'd gotten from the Bird's Eye Bakery when someone rang my doorbell.

I glanced around the room. "Is anyone expecting company?"

Everyone shook their heads and I let out a sigh as I went to the front door. If it was any of the coven members, they'd have called or texted first. That meant it was either a door-to-door marketer or—I cut off my thoughts when I spotted the bubble lights of a police car through the window.

Trouble had just arrived.

"What the hell?" Jax asked as he stepped beside me.

"No idea. There's only one way to find out, though." I reached for the front door and pulled it open.

Officer Stone stood on the front porch with a hardened expression on his face. "Is Jax Williams here?"

I glanced over at Jax and said, "Yes. Why?"

"The PPPD has questions for both of you. May we come in?" Stone asked, his voice all business.

"Is this about Fiona's water line?" I demanded. "Because neither of us know who cut it. We've told you that already."

"It's not about that." Stone didn't wait for me to extend

the invitation. He just pushed past me and walked right in. Wallis followed, looking somber.

"What's happened?" I asked, suddenly concerned. These two cops had lost their sneers and sarcasm. Something serious must have gone down.

"Lacey Riley has gone missing," Stone said, producing a picture of the woman Kai had saved from her abusive partner at the beach a couple of days ago.

"What?" I cried. "When? How?"

"Where were you earlier today at around 1:00 p.m.?" Wallis asked.

"Me?" I gasped out. "I was here, cleaning my house before our company came over."

"Can anyone corroborate your story?" Wallis asked.

I glanced down at Minx. "I'm guessing you can't take the word of a Chihuahua?"

He didn't respond. Not even a tiny flinch.

"Nobody else was home, but it's possible a neighbor saw me watering my plants." I narrowed my eyes at him. "But why would I be a suspect? I don't even know her. The other day at the beach was the first time I'd ever met her."

"Just covering our bases, ma'am." Stone looked at Jax. "And you?"

"Today at one?" He frowned. "I was with Sawyer Davies. He's the foreman for my construction business. I'd guess we were on our way to lunch at Pointe of View Café."

"You guess? You don't know?" The cop's tone was full of skepticism.

"It's not like I was keeping a log of the time today. I left here at about twelve thirty, met him at the office, and then we went to lunch."

"And after lunch?"

"We went over to the Gray Wolf Winery to discuss a job Kai has hired us to do." Stone stiffened and looked up from his notes with ice in his gaze. "You were with Kai Gray? What time?"

A pit formed in my stomach. I just knew that if there was a way for the Premonition Pointe police department to pin this on Kai, and possibly Jax, they would.

Jax shrugged. "About two or three o'clock maybe? Again, I wasn't logging the time."

"How was Mr. Gray when you saw him?" Wallis asked.

"What do you mean exactly?" Jax asked.

Stone had leaned against my couch, making himself comfortable. Then he leaned forward and asked, "Did he seem agitated? Nervous? Unusual in any way?"

Wallis seemed to vibrate with anticipation. It disgusted me that these two officers were salivating for any hint of incriminating evidence that Kai might be involved in the disappearance of Lacey.

"No." Jax crossed his arms over his chest and glared at them. "I discussed building a barn at the winery with Mr. Gray, and that's all I have to say about it."

"Just a few more question, Mr. Williams," Stone said, ignoring Jax's obvious dismissal. "How would you describe Mr. Gray's character when he's in wolf form?"

"I'm not answering any more questions." Jax stepped over to the door and yanked it open. "You can leave now."

Stone and Wallis both glared at him but made no move toward my door.

"I'm sure you don't want to make enemies of us, Mr. Williams," Stone said evenly.

"It kind of looks like I might already have," Jax said, his knuckles turning white as he gripped the edge of the door. "So unless you have some grounds to arrest me, I suggest you leave now. You're on private property, Officer Stone. I'm sure you're aware of that."

"Jax is right," I agreed. "And you interrupted our family dinner, so I'd appreciate it if you'd go now. We don't know anything about this case, so you're wasting your time anyway." I felt rather than saw Charlotte and Ty move to stand behind me. And although the last thing I wanted was an altercation with two of Premonition Pointe's police officers, I appreciated the support.

After a long moment, Stone finally stood. He walked to the door, but just before he and Wallis left, he stared me right in the eye. "If I were you, Ms. Matched, I'd be a lot more careful about who I chose to spend my time with."

I crossed my arms over my chest and glared at him but didn't respond.

Finally, the two walked out and Jax slammed the door behind them.

Everyone started to talk at once while I walked over to the couch and sank into the cushions. Jax stood behind me and placed his hands on my shoulders, rubbing gently.

"Don't worry, Marion," he whispered in my ear. "There are plenty of witnesses that will confirm Sawyer and I were at lunch during the time Lacey went missing."

I glanced back at him. "Yeah, I know. But we both have to face the fact that those two are going to do everything they can to pin this on you, Kai, or one of his pack, and it's all because you're shifters. Not because there's any actual evidence that any of you would do something like this."

He kneaded my muscles, pressing harder than usual, and I had to place my hands over his to get him to ease up. "Sorry. You're right, but I don't know what we can do about that."

"I do," Charlotte interjected.

All of us turned our attention to her. I scoffed. "What's that? Cast some sort of spell to eliminate their bigotry?"

That made her chuckle. "I wish. If there was a spell that did that, I'd open a business pronto and get to work ridding the world of such hatred."

"You'd be mega rich," Denver said as he reached down and picked up Minx, who'd just started yapping her approval of Charlotte's plan.

"That'd just be a nice perk," Charlotte said wistfully. Then she sighed and looked at me. "No, I'm not proposing a spell. We just need to find out what happened to Lacey and prove that Jax, Kai, and the pack had nothing to do with it."

"You're suggesting we get involved in the investigation?" I asked.

Charlotte rolled her eyes at me. "Of course. We've done it before. Why not now?"

She had a point. In fact, the more I thought about it, the more I wondered why I hadn't come up with that solution first. "You know what, Charlotte? I think I'm rubbing off on you."

My sister scoffed. "No way. If anything, it's me who's having an effect on you." She scanned my body, and when she got to my shoes, she smirked. "Look at how stylish those heels are. When I arrived, you were wearing those hippy sandals... with socks."

Everyone started to laugh.

I placed my hands on my hips and shook my head. "No, I wasn't. I don't even own any of those sandals."

"Only because you 'lost' them after I threw them out," she insisted.

I couldn't help the laughter escaping from my lips. While she was flat out lying, which we both knew, it was true that since she'd come to town, I'd upped my fashion game a little. I'd also been booking regular appointments at the spa to keep my hair dyed and my upper lip waxed... at least before Jax disappeared on me.

When everyone was quiet again, I held my sister's gaze and said, "I like your plan. Should we start tomorrow?"

"I'm in," she said.

"Marion—" Jax started, worry in his tone.

I held my hand up, stopping him. "I know you'd rather I stay out of this, but I'm not taking any chances. You're working with Kai now and you're part of their circle. If something goes down and you get caught up in it, I don't know what I'll do. Besides, someone needs to be on the pack's side. If the police are this hostile to them, what will happen when the rest of the town learns Kai and the pack are their main 'suspects'? It will make their lives hell, and they don't deserve that."

Ty, who'd been silent the entire time, finally spoke up. "Marion, how well do you know Kai? Are you sure he didn't have anything to do with this?"

"Not you, too?" I asked, astonished that Ty would buy into the cop's narrative.

"It's not that—" He flopped down on the couch next to me and ran a hand through his dark hair. "Listen. I'm not saying that Kai or the pack had anything to do with this, and the bigotry is disgusting. I just want to make sure you're not putting your neck on the line for someone we don't even know that well."

"You mean like you did for Carson?" I asked with one raised eyebrow.

"That's... different," he stammered. "He's my brother."

"One you didn't even know."

Ty didn't answer.

I studied him, frowning. "Why does it matter if we don't know him that well? Isn't standing up for those who are being discriminated against just the right thing to do?"

"Arg!" Ty let out a cry of frustration. "Of course it is. But why does it always have to be you?" He kept his gaze on the floor when he said, "I already lost one mother. I don't want to lose another one."

Even though he hadn't technically lost Trish, I knew what he meant. While what I planned to do wasn't even remotely close to being the same stunt she'd pulled, I could see why he'd be concerned. In the past when I'd repeatedly put myself on the line to help others, usually they were people close to me, the ones I loved most. Not someone I'd just met. "You're not going to lose me, Ty. Not ever. Charlotte and I are just going to do what we can to see who else might be a suspect. Give the police another angle so they'll stop harassing Jax and Kai."

He gave me a skeptical look.

I just shrugged. What could I say? It wasn't like I'd never gotten into a pickle a time or two before.

Kennedy came and sat next to Ty, holding his hand. "If Marion didn't help where she could, she wouldn't be Marion."

Ty looked at him, let out another sigh, and said, "You're right of course." Then he looked at me again. "Just be careful, okay, Mama Marion?"

I wrapped an arm around his shoulders and gave him a sideways hug. "I absolutely will be careful. I promise."

"Famous last words," Charlotte muttered.

"You're not helping," I said.

She just beamed at me. "Where do we start?"

CHAPTER 10

"First things first." I looked up at Jax. "Ty has a point; I don't know Kai that well. All I have is the background check we run on all our clients. There weren't any red flags. The worst thing was a blip on his credit, which I understand was because of his ex. What's your take on him? I see him as a thoughtful and caring leader to his pack. He seems like a really solid guy to me. What about you?"

Jax nodded. "I get the same impression. He's tough but fair. Charming when he wants to be. He certainly doesn't have trouble attracting attention from the female population."

"Ted Bundy was charming, too," Celia chimed in, startling me as she appeared in the chair across from us.

I shook my head at her. "Was that necessary?"

"What? Pointing out the obvious?" She buffed her fingernails. "But Jax is right. That Kai is one serious hunk of manmeat. I don't mind keeping an eye on him if you want to know what's really going on over there at the winery."

"That's a good idea," Ty said, nodding.

"It's settled then. I'll surveil the alpha and report back." Celia disappeared again with a loud pop.

Jax frowned at Ty and then at me. "You're really going to let her spy on the pack? That's awfully invasive, don't you think?"

"I don't *let* her do anything. Celia does whatever she wants. You know that," I said.

Jax was clearly irritated when he said, "They haven't done anything to warrant being spied on. I just don't think it's right." He glanced at Ty again. "You shouldn't have encouraged her."

Ty visibly swallowed and then grimaced. "You're right. I'm just worried about Marion is all. I didn't think it through."

"I'll keep whatever she finds confidential. And I'll do my best to make sure Celia doesn't go blabbing about anything she finds," I said. "While I can't control her, I do have some sway."

Jax nodded, but still had a frown on his face.

"Is something going on with Celia and Danny?" Charlotte asked. "She seemed awfully eager to spend her time spying on the new Alpha in town."

"I don't think so," I said, shaking my head. "You know Celia, always wanting to be in the thick of things."

"Always wanting to spy on good-looking men, you mean," Charlotte replied.

"True." I couldn't argue with that. Celia was a little sex obsessed. The entire reason she was in my life at all was because she'd hired me to be her matchmaker and then died in a tragic accident while on her way to her date. After her unfortunate demise, she showed up demanding I set her up with someone in her afterlife since her date had moved on with someone else. She'd been desperate for a ghostly boyfriend of her own.

"Jax, what else do you know about Kai? Anything that should give us pause?" I asked.

He shook his head. "Not that I can think of, but honestly, I don't know him all that well. I mostly kept to myself when I was working out my wolf side." He glanced away, and I knew he didn't want to talk about it.

"You should call my mom," Ty said. "She's known him longer."

I stared at him. "Are you sure you want her here?"

"If it will keep you safe, then yes." Ty stood up and held his hand out to Kennedy. "Thanks for dinner, Marion. I think Kennedy and I will take Paris Francine on a walk."

As the pair said their goodbyes, I stood and gave Ty a hug. "Love you."

"Love you, too," he whispered back.

When they were gone, I called Trish.

A half hour later, my former best friend walked in. She glanced around. "Ty isn't here?"

"No, he and Kennedy were here for dinner, but they've already left for the evening," I said, not sure why I was giving details. Maybe just to let her know that he was doing okay.

"I see." She looked defeated but added, "I was hoping to say hello."

"That's not a good idea," Charlotte interjected. "Give the

man some space, Trish. He's already said he'd call you when he's ready to talk. Stop smothering him. It'll only push him away further."

I gave my sister a grateful smile. We both had mother issues of our own that we'd had to work through, so I was certain her words came from a place of deep understanding.

Trish threw her an irritated glance. "Of course I'm not going to bother him. He's made it abundantly clear he's not ready to talk to me. I got it, okay?" Then she stood by the door with her arms crossed over her chest. "What is this about Kai and the pack being targeted by the police?"

"Why don't you have a seat?" I asked.

She shook her head. "I'm fine here."

I suppressed a sigh and quickly explained the situation with the missing woman and how the police were already set to blame Kai despite any actual evidence, circumstantial or otherwise.

Trish frowned, looking deeply troubled. "Kai is as solid as they come. Not once have I ever seen him even act aggressive toward a female... at least not one who wasn't in wolf form while he was defending the pack. I also haven't ever even gotten that vibe off him." She met my gaze. "You know, the one that just gives you the *ick*, that says someone is a threat even when they haven't really done anything you can pinpoint."

I nodded, knowing exactly what she meant. "That's good. So bottom line, you don't think Kai could have abducted Lacey?"

"No way." She shook her head. "I'd swear on that."

"Good." I glanced at Charlotte. "So we start investigating tomorrow?"

"Yep."

I made a mental note to remember to talk to the coven about casting a spell to find Lacey and then got up and walked over to Trish. "Thanks for coming. I appreciate it."

"Sure. I don't want to see anything happen to the pack. While I have no plans to formally join any pack, I do sort of consider myself one of them now. It's not right what the PPPD is doing to them."

We all agreed.

Trish was on her way out when the door opened and Ty walked in, looking a little conflicted. His brows were drawn down, and he was picking at the hem of his T-shirt. But there was also a steadfastness to him when he looked at his mother and said, "You didn't come to the apartment or text me."

"You asked me not to," she said warily.

"That's true. I did," he said with a nod. "And honestly, if you had, I wouldn't be here right now."

Trish raised both eyebrows and tentatively asked, "Does that mean you're ready to talk now?"

"I think so." He looked at Kennedy, who gave him a nod of encouragement. "Can we start with lunch once a week? An hour or so on Tuesdays?"

Relief seemed to wash over Trish as she smiled at him. "Yes. I'd love to do that."

"Good. I'll text you with a time and place." He reached for Kennedy, and just like that they were gone again.

Trish turned to me. "Did you know he was going to do that?"

I shook my head, just as surprised as she was. "Nope. But he was the one who suggested I call you earlier." I knew that

Ty was seeing a therapist, and the lunch idea was something she'd suggested. A neutral place for Ty and his mother to meet and try to build something new, rather than go back to old patterns from when Ty was still a teenager. But I hadn't known he was seriously considering it.

Trish sighed. "He's so different now. The boy I knew would never have behaved so distantly."

I did my best to be diplomatic when I answered. "He's a grown man now, Trish. He's grown up a lot in the past five years. He's not the teenager you remember anymore." I wanted to add that he'd also recently learned that everything he thought to be true about his family was basically a lie and she couldn't expect him to just get over it, but I kept that part to myself.

"I know that," she said, looking sad. "I just didn't expect to be walking around with a giant hole in my heart after being reunited with him. I honestly thought I was doing what was best for him at the time. Sometimes I still do, but we'll never know, and I can't change it now."

"I know you did," I said, trying to suppress my own resentment at mourning her for five years. I could have handled her secret, but she hadn't trusted me either, and that still hurt even though I knew she wasn't trying to cause any of us pain. "It was a bad situation, and maybe there wasn't a right answer. All we can do is move forward."

"Yeah. I better go." Trish started to reach for the doorhandle and paused. "Marion?"

"Yeah?"

"I'm sorry I hurt you."

Her words hung in the air. It was the first time she'd apologized that made me feel like she truly understood what we'd all gone through when we thought we'd lost her. It was a glimpse of the Trish I used to know, and I felt hopeful that maybe, just maybe, we'd find a way to get back to the friendship we had before she'd gone missing. "Thank you. I'm sorry you thought you had to make that choice."

Trish nodded and silently slipped out the door.

Charlotte and Denver stayed for a while longer after Trish left, but eventually they stood and Charlotte called for Minx. "Come on girl. We're staying the night at Denver's."

Minx just looked at her and then sat down stubbornly at Jax's feet.

"You little turncoat," Charlotte said with a soft chuckle. "Come on now, you can't stay here all the time. Aunty Marion is going to get tired of all this dogsitting she does for free."

Minx hopped up and ran around to stand behind Jax, barely poking her nose out to see if Charlotte was going to force her hand.

Charlotte sighed while Denver chuckled softly. "Stop it," Charlotte told him. "I've lost my true love to my sister's boyfriend. It's not fair."

Denver rolled his eyes at her. "Minx just missed him."

Jax reached down and scooped up the pup, who was wearing a red and white polka dot dress. "She can stay with me if it's okay with you, Charlotte. I missed her too."

"Fine," Charlotte said with a huff. She walked over to Jax and Minx, giving the dog a kiss on her head. "But tomorrow is spa day, little girl. I'll be back by eight to pick you up."

Minx wagged her tail vigorously as if she understood every word Charlotte had said and then snuggled into Jax's chest.

Denver was still laughing as the pair left.

I looked at my boyfriend and the dog who was stealing all his affection. "I've lost you, haven't I?"

He grinned. "Just until she passes out. Then I'm all yours."

Minx yawned right on cue, and we both chuckled.

"Come on," I said, tugging him toward the bedroom. "I'm next in line for those snuggles."

CHAPTER 11

*W*hen we were finally tucked into my bed, I rolled over and laid on Jax's chest. Minx was on his other side, curled up next to him. We were the picture of domestic bliss, and it made me think about our conversation when we were at Fiona's and he'd brought up marriage. "Jax?"

"Hmm?" He ran his hand through my hair lazily.

"Are you really considering marriage?" It had been on my mind, but I hadn't really known how to bring it up.

Jax stiffened, making me lift my head to stare down at him.

"What is it?" I asked. "I'm not looking for a proposal if that's what's got you freaked out. I just want to know where your head's at."

He groaned and glanced away before meeting my eyes again. "It's not that. I just…" He closed his eyes briefly and shook his head. "Before I was bitten, I thought that one day we'd probably get married. Maybe after the house on the beach was built. But now…" He grimaced. "I don't know if it's fair to ask that of you."

"Fair?" My voice was a few octaves higher than normal. "What does that even mean?"

"You know. I'd be asking you to sign up for this." He waved a hand, indicating himself.

I snorted a laugh. "Well, obviously."

"I mean, you'd be signing up to spend the rest of your life with a wolf shifter. I don't know if it's right to ask that of you."

"It's no worse than asking you to deal with a witch," I countered. He opened his mouth, and I could tell he was going to protest. I placed my hand over his lips and said, "Let's not worry about any of that, okay? We haven't even been dating a year. And after all the changes in our lives these last few months, I don't think either of us are ready to get married. So there's no reason to make that sort of decision now. But I will tell you that when I think about my future, you're always in it. And I do see rings eventually. I'm not going anywhere. Is that enough for now?"

His face brightened as he smiled up at me. "It's enough. Definitely enough."

"Good. Now kiss me. I've missed your lips."

"Since this morning?" he asked, looking amused.

"Yes."

In one swift motion, he grabbed me and flipped us so that I was lying on my back and Jax was hovering over me. And then without a word, he gave me a whole lot more than just a kiss.

~

"WHAT'S WRONG?" Aunt Lucy asked when she picked up the call on the first ring.

"Why do you think something's wrong?" I asked as I poured cream into my coffee. It was Monday morning, just before eight. Normally I wouldn't call anyone that early, but I knew my aunt was an early riser. She'd likely gotten up with the sun.

"You almost never call before lunch time."

"True. But I had you on my mind and wanted to see when we can get everyone together for dinner. I missed you and Dad last night."

"Oh, we missed you, too. You should have been there, Marion. It was the best time."

"The card tournament?" I asked, trying to hide my skepticism. I liked playing cards, but the idea of meeting up for a tournament with a bunch of strangers made me cringe.

"Yes. We played a game called Rage. It was a blast, but the best part was the company. There was a woman who inherited her granddaddy's honeybee farm recently. I guess she grows a bunch of lavender, too. She and Tazia bonded immediately."

"I can see that." Tazia, who happened to be my neighbor and was dating my father, owned a floral business in town. She'd definitely be interested in someone who was in the honey and lavender business.

"Even Memphis liked her, and you know how he can be sometimes. Anyway, Fiona is a riot. We can't wait to go back next week."

"Fiona?" I repeated. Premonition Pointe wasn't a large town. The odds of there being two Fionas were low. Plus, Fiona Fitzgerald did have a large piece of property. We hadn't looked around, but it certainly looked like she had plenty of acreage for bees and a lavender farm. "Fiona Fitzgerald?"

"Yes! That's her. Do you know her?" Lucy asked.

"We've met." I paused, remembering the miserable woman who'd berated Kai and Jax over the broken water line. I couldn't imagine her mustering up even five minutes of delightfulness.

"Don't you just love her?" Lucy continued to gush.

"I'm not sure we had enough interaction for me to form an opinion," I lied. "I'll just have to take your word for it."

"Maybe we'll get you down to Hallucinations and you can see for yourself," Lucy said.

Doubtful. "Maybe. Hey, listen, Jax and I need to get going, but what about Saturday night? Are you and Gael free for family dinner? Hopefully with Dad and Tazia, too. I still have to call him." Gael was her boyfriend, and ever since they'd started dating, Aunt Lucy had been happier than ever.

"Saturday? Yeah, that should work. I'll tell your dad. Are you cooking or are we going out?"

"Thanks. I'll cook," I said, already wondering if I should just get takeout. If Ty and Kennedy and Charlotte and Denver also came, I'd be cooking for ten.

"Perfect. I'll bring dessert."

We said our goodbyes and I was just ending the call when Jax walked into the kitchen. He glanced at the coffee in my hand and said, "I thought we were headed out for breakfast."

"We are. I just needed a quick shot of caffeine first."

He reached out and took the mug from me. After he took a long sip, he handed it back. "Thanks."

"Sure." I downed the rest of it. "Let's go. I'm starving."

"After last night, I'm not surprised," he teased.

I felt my cheeks flush. Ever since he'd come home, we hadn't been able to keep our hands off each other.

Jax followed me to the Pointe of View Café. After breakfast, he was heading to his office, and I was meeting Charlotte at the dating agency so we could get to work on finding out what might have happened to Lacey.

"Thanks for taking the time to have breakfast with me," I said as we were being seated by the hostess.

He paused to kiss the top of my head before he sat across from me. "I wouldn't miss this for anything. Do you have any idea how long it's been since I've had those chocolate, peanut butter, whipped cream waffles they make?"

"I'm guessing a little over six weeks," I said, doing my best to keep the grimace off my face. The very idea of loading up with sugar and carbs for breakfast made me instantly crave a nap.

"Don't worry. I won't make you eat it," he said with a chuckle.

I smirked at him, shaking my head. "How is it you always know what I'm thinking?"

"I know you, Marion Matched."

The waitress arrived with coffee and took our orders.

Once she retreated, Jax grinned at me. "Avocado toast?"

"What's wrong with that?" I asked.

"Nothing. I could have bet cash money that's what you would get. See, Marion? I really do know you."

I liked this playful version of Jax. Ever since he'd been bitten by that wolf, he'd carried a cloud of darkness. But he seemed to have shed that gloom and was coming back to himself. I reached across the table and squeezed his hand.

"Jax? Marion?" a familiar male voice called.

I glanced up to see Kai headed straight for us and raised my hand in greeting. "Morning."

"Hey, Kai." Jax waved to the empty chair beside him. "Take a seat."

The haggard-looking alpha took him up on the offer and eyed my coffee cup.

I guarded it protectively as I waved at the waitress to get her attention and then pointed at Kai and my coffee cup. She hurried over, and Kai gave her a grateful smile.

"Rough night?" I asked.

Kai sucked down half the contents of his mug before he answered. "You could say that. I guess you heard about Lacey going missing."

"We did," Jax said. "We also got the impression the PPPD is looking to pin that on you."

"Ludicrous, isn't it? I don't know why they aren't looking at her ex. That John guy. There's a reason she has a restraining order against him," Kai said with a scoff.

I frowned. "Wasn't he arrested? I assumed he was in custody."

"Not according to my sources," Kai said, holding his cup of coffee with both hands. "He was released in less than twenty-four hours."

"Are you sure they aren't looking into him?" Jax asked, his expression troubled.

Kai gave him a half shrug. "I can't be positive, but I do know someone with some insider knowledge. Unless they are lying or have been lied to, then no, they aren't looking at him. The detectives think he left town as soon as he was released."

"And they haven't followed up?" I gasped out.

"Not that I'm aware of," Kai said.

"Well, that changes everything doesn't it?" Anger surged through my veins. This was starting to look more and more like a specific vendetta against Kai and the pack. "That's just downright irresponsible. If John was looking to abduct Lacey, wouldn't it make sense to put the cops off his trail and make it look like he left?"

"Any thinking person would check in to that," Jax agreed.

"They would if they cared at all about justice." Kai's tone was matter of fact as if he'd witnessed this scenario before. It made me all the more outraged.

"We'll just have to *make* them care," I said. "I'll have my guy run background checks on both Lacey and John and see if we can catch any leads on where John might be."

Kai stared at me, looking perplexed.

"What?"

"Why would you do that? Go out of your way to find information on them?" Kai asked.

I frowned. "Why wouldn't I?"

"Because most people don't like to get involved." He clutched his mug tightly when he added, "Especially when it involves wolves."

I let out a small huff. "If you haven't noticed, I'm pretty

attached to my wolf." I slid my hand over Jax's and squeezed. "Plus, it's just wrong the way the PPPD is treating you. Someone has to stand up for you guys." I gave him a teasing smile. "Just consider it part of my service. I can't have one of my most eligible bachelors being framed for an abduction, now can I?"

"So you're basically saying you'll do anything for love?" he quipped.

Jax snorted a laugh.

I grinned at Kai. "Something like that." But then I sobered as the image of the boy they'd saved from the waves a few days before flashed through my mind. "Do you happen to know where Cody is?" The idea that John may have abducted that little boy made my stomach turn.

"Cody is with his grandmother. Apparently somewhere up north," Kai said. "My contact was able to tell me that much but nothing more specific. And honestly, I don't want to know. The less I'm connected to this the better. If we end up in court, I don't want to have to testify that I was checking into his whereabouts."

Relief rushed through me, but my heart also broke for what Cody must be going through with his mother missing. I prayed his grandmother's home was a safe and loving environment. He was going to need it.

"You don't need to look into anything," I reassured Kai. "My sister and I are on it. Plus, I have a coven as backup."

He blinked at me, clearly shocked. "I can't ask you to do that."

"You didn't ask. And you can't stop me either," I said with a smirk.

Jax chuckled. "That's true."

"The cops aren't going to find anything connecting me or the pack to this," Kai said. "I think, for now, it's better if we just see where this goes. I've already called my lawyer. He can handle it."

I could see why Kai was willing to let it ride. He'd probably been dealing with this type of discrimination his entire wolf existence. It seemed obvious to me that his strategy was to make nice, be helpful, and eventually break through people's bigotry. And while I certainly admired that approach, I couldn't just sit back and do nothing about Lacey. Nor could I put up with a police force that was so blatantly bigoted that they would sacrifice a woman's safety just to take down someone they hated for no justifiable reason. But was it the entire police force, or did Stone and Wallis have a personal beef with Kai?

"That's probably a good plan," I told Kai. Then I gave him a small smile. "But I'm still going to do what I have to do."

"I can't talk you out of it?" Kai asked.

"You can try, but you won't get anywhere," Jax said. "Let's just say that backing down isn't in her nature."

I chuckled softly. Jax was right. When I was determined, backing down wasn't an option. Not today. Not ever.

"Hey, Kai?" I asked.

He glanced up from his coffee.

"Have you had any interactions with Stone or Wallis before this? Is there a reason they'd be coming after you for something?"

"You think they might be targeting me for something other than just being a wolf?" he asked curiously.

"Maybe? I don't know. Just thinking out loud."

He shook his head. "No. As far as I know, I've never met them before moving to Premonition Pointe."

"So they just have a bug up their ass. Got it," I quipped.

As Jax and Kai chuckled, I decided it was time to visit the Premonition Pointe police chief.

CHAPTER 12

"I guess your plan to save the business from ruin is in the toilet now, huh?" Charlotte said as she stared at her computer and shook her head.

"Why do you say that?" I asked as I placed my purse in one of my drawers. I'd just walked in and found her already at her desk.

"An anonymous post is making the rounds today on all the Premonition Pointe social media spaces, claiming that Kai is the main suspect in the disappearance of Lacey Riley. People are calling for him and the pack to be run out of town."

"What?" I hurried over to her desk and looked over her shoulder. There was comment after comment from people claiming that Kai and his pack gave them "bad vibes." Another one demanded that the wolves be rounded up and given their own lands far away from society. That one had over a hundred likes already. Groaning, I sat heavily on the edge of her desk and buried my face in my hands. When I lifted my head, I muttered, "This is a disaster."

"People have definitely lost their minds," she agreed. "But I'm sure we can find someone else for Autumn to date so we don't get canceled again."

"Huh?" It took a moment to process what my sister was saying. Then I shook my head. "No. Kai and Autumn are a perfect match. You saw their auras together."

"I did, but—"

"No, Charlotte. I'm not going to change my matches just so it looks good to the public. We'll find another way to turn things around."

"Okay, if you say so," she said with a shrug.

"I do. Now let's try to find out who really abducted Lacey Riley. If we get that solved, we can clear Kai and the pack and move on."

"I'm down. What do you want me to do?" She sat at attention waiting for orders.

"Do a social media check online. See what you can find out about Lacey Riley and her ex, John Vincent. Pay attention to anything that might help us with her whereabouts in the past week or two."

She nodded once and got to work.

I took a moment to once again marvel at the change in my sister. When she'd first arrived in Premonition Pointe, she was entitled and petulant. We hadn't gotten off to a great start at all. But over the last months, she'd become someone I enjoyed working with and having around on a regular basis.

"Stop looking at me like that," she said without looking up.

"I'm not looking at you," I lied as I strode to my desk and picked up the phone.

"Sure you weren't."

I ignored her remark and dialed Sebastian Knight. He was an attorney who also had contacts that provided the most thorough background checks one could hope for. He was also the partner of my coven mate Gigi Martin. It was nice to have connections.

Once Sebastian confirmed he'd get the results to me as soon as possible, I hung up and called Brix. He was the Magical Task Force agent who Charlotte and I worked for when he needed us on a case. After we'd discovered that when we combined our magic together we were more powerful than even the highest-ranking MTF agents, Brix talked us into working for the agency. I'd agreed, but only if we were working for him. My experiences with law enforcement had left me with far too many trust issues. Too many of them were corrupt. But Brix was different. He was one of the good guys.

"Marion Matched," Brix said when he answered. "Tell me this is a social call and you're not cursed by black magic that's going to turn you into a demon by sundown."

"That was... specific," I said, shaking my head in amusement. "Tell me you aren't in the middle of saving someone from demonism."

He laughed. "It's not that dire. If it were, I'd have called you."

"You know what? I don't think you're joking," I said, trying to ignore the mental images of someone slowly turning into a demon.

"I'm not. What's up, Marion? Do you need backup on something?"

I loved that Brix trusted me and would send reinforcements with no questions asked. He trusted that Charlotte and I weren't out there using our power to cause trouble. He knew we'd only tap into that kind of power if we absolutely needed to.

"Not backup exactly," I said. "But we do seem to have a discrimination problem here in Premonition Pointe. And it all started with the PPPD."

"Discrimination? Against who?"

"Wolf shifters," I said, my skin heating with anger all over again. I quickly filled Brix in on the abduction and how Premonition Pointe's finest seemed laser-focused on Kai instead of looking for actual leads.

"Damn," he muttered. "As you know, I don't have any official jurisdiction over the town police department, but I can file a complaint that will open an investigation. Does this have anything to do with Jax?"

"They did question him, but so far, they've backed off. Kai is the one in their crosshairs. I was thinking about going down there to talk to the chief to find out if it's a problem within the entire department, or just the two officers that questioned us and Kai."

"Hmm, let me check on the police chief. If it's the entire department, we don't need them coming for you, too. I'll get back to you as soon as I know anything," he said. "Meanwhile, keep me updated on what you learn about the case, okay?"

Goddess, I adored that man. He was always coming through when I needed him. My lips twitched with amusement as I asked, "You just assumed I'd be investigating?"

"Aren't you?"

"Yes."

He chuckled. "That's what I thought. Take care of yourself, Marion. I'll be in touch."

As soon as I ended the call, Charlotte poked her head out from behind her computer monitor and said, "Come here. I think I've found something."

I prayed it was something good. Or at least something that would give us a starting point. When I was perched over her shoulder, she pointed at her screen.

"Look at this."

I squinted and reached for my reading glasses that were on the top of my head. Once I could actually see the screen, I noted that she was on Lacey's Facebook page. There was a post of her in overalls and holding up a pair of boots. The caption said, "On my way to lock this job down! Wish me luck." It was tagged #farmerlife #manifesting #sendgoodvibes.

"So she went to a job interview a couple of days ago? And she went missing yesterday, right?" I asked.

"This post is from day before yesterday," Charlotte confirmed. "A few days before that, she mentioned looking for a job, any job, and she asked people to respond if they knew anyone hiring." Charlotte scrolled up. "See here? One of her friends asked what she's looking for, and she said anything with a decent wage, but she really wanted a job at a nursery or somewhere that she could be outside and work with nature. This person listed a few places, and Lacey liked the comment."

"Write those down," I said as I went to my own computer and started looking at job notices that were posted on the town website. I didn't see any specifically for nurseries, but there were a few for some of the downtown stores, including Sky's the Limit, a designer clothing boutique owned by Skyler Cole. Carson, Ty's half brother, worked there as a junior designer. I made my own list and then stood, grabbing my purse. "These places give us a starting point. Ready to go knock on some doors?"

"Where are you headed?" Celia asked just before she popped into the office.

"To find out if anyone knows anything about Lacey or saw her before her disappearance," I said a little impatiently. "What are you up to?"

"Absolutely nothing," Celia said with a dramatic sigh before she slowly blinked her big Kewpie doll eyes. "I have been hanging out at that winery since last night, and you know what I found out?"

"What?" Charlotte asked as she put her sweater on. It was still pretty foggy on the coast, so I grabbed mine as well.

"Kai Gray is the most *boring* wolf I've ever had the displeasure of spying on." She made a sour face and added, "If it wasn't for that eight pack of abs he's sporting, I'd have plucked my eyes out last night just for something to do."

"Boring? You mean there's really nothing to report?" I asked her, relieved that my instincts had been on point.

"Not unless you want to know that he watches *Star Trek* before bed, takes about twenty minutes to brush his teeth, and has his vitamins all organized in a daily pill container. Man, I swear he's more like a ninety-year-old man rather than a sexy fifty-ish shifter. Those fiction books just can't be trusted. I was expecting him to see me hovering over him and then ravage me all night. Instead, I got soft snoring and a foot twitch that made me think he was dreaming of chasing rabbits."

I cackled at her description. "Did you really think he was going to ravage a ghost?"

"I don't know. It's what would happen if there was any justice in this world," she insisted. "He's too effing hot for his boring-old-man routine."

"What about Danny?" Charlotte asked. "Are you two on the outs?"

"No," she said, looking perplexed. "Why would you ask that?"

"Never mind." Charlotte shook her head and then tied her long red hair up into a ponytail.

"You can lay off spying on the Alpha, Celia," I told the ghost. "It's invasive, and we don't have any reason to suspect him of anything. Why don't you go down to Abs, Buns, and Guns and see what kind of trouble you can get into?"

"You know, I think I just might. If Danny is there, I'll give him a little show. Toodles!" She waved her fingers and disappeared again.

"Toodles." Charlotte chuckled softly. "She's always good for some fresh entertainment."

"No doubt," I agreed and then led the way out the door.

CHAPTER 13

"*W*ho's first?" I asked Charlotte, who had both lists of potential employers.

"I figured it would be best to try the two places that were recommended to Lacey first," Charlotte said, peering at her notebook.

"I agree. Which one?" We were in my SUV, the vehicle idling in the parking space until I knew which direction to go.

"Chick-A-Daze and Happy Hollow," Charlotte said, opening the map app on her phone. "Looks like both are south of town, inland a little bit."

"Okay." I pulled out of the parking spot and headed for 101 South. "Can you find any info on those places?"

"Sure. Chick-A-Daze has a Facebook page. Along with having a Christmas tree farm, it says they raise designer chickens and have a seasonal pumpkin patch."

"Christmas trees, pumpkins, and chickens. Interesting," I said with a chuckle.

"*Designer* chickens, whatever that means," Charlotte said.

"I'm now envisioning chickens wearing Alexander McQueen or Coco Chanel. Maybe some Jimmy Choos to go along with their fine threads?"

Charlotte blinked at me and then started laughing so hard she had trouble breathing. "That's not an image I'm going to get out of my head anytime soon."

"Me neither to be honest."

We were still amused when we turned into the long, gravel driveway of Chick-A-Daze Farm. There was a large overgrown field to the north and at the fork in the drive, there was signage indicating the pumpkin field was to the south and the tree farm to the east.

Charlotte let out a noise of disapproval. "Look at all those weeds in the gravel. And that field looks like it hasn't been tended in a month."

"No wonder they were looking for help," I said. When we pulled up to the main house, the place didn't look like it was rundown, just that the occupants were having trouble keeping up with the fall maintenance.

As we were climbing out of the SUV, the front door swung open and a woman wearing jeans, a black T-shirt, and a red apron stepped out onto the porch as she wiped her hands on a white linen cloth. "You missed the sign to the pumpkin patch. Turn around and go left at the fork in the road."

"Sorry to bother you ma'am. We're not here for the pumpkins. We were hoping to ask you a few questions," I said.

The gray-haired woman, crossed her arms over her chest and asked, "About?"

I gave her a pleasant smile. "I'm Marion, and this is my sister, Charlotte."

The woman stared at me with impatience, and I realized she must have thought we were door-to-door solicitors and she resented being interrupted.

"Sorry to interrupt your day," I said. "We saw online that your operation might be hiring and—"

"If you want a job interview, you'll need to make an appointment with my daughter. I don't handle that." She started to move to go back into the house.

"Wait!" I called. "We're not looking for a job. We're looking for information about a young woman who may have come for a job interview a couple of days ago. Lacey Riley?"

"What's it to you?" The gray-haired woman glared at me like I'd just insulted her favorite dog.

"She's gone missing, and we're trying to retrace her steps to see if we can get an idea of what happened to her," I rushed out.

"Oh. Missing. I see." The older woman softened for just a moment before stiffening again. "Ask those wolves. I bet they know what happened to her."

"Wolves?" I asked, my heart racing. Had the PPPD brainwashed everyone in this town already? How did she even know about the Diablo wolf pack? Their establishment was nearly twenty miles away in the opposite direction of her farm.

"Yes, wolves. Ever since they came to town, our chickens have been going missing. I just know it's them. Coming here in the middle of the night to feast on our precious babies. They should be run out of town on a rail."

As if on cue, the faint sounds of chickens squawking could be heard from behind the house.

"Do you have any video proof?" I asked her, though I didn't believe for a minute that the wolves were coming all the way down to her farm for live chickens.

"No," she spat. "The night they raided the coop, the power was cut to our place, and we don't have even one video clip." She opened her front door, reached in, and pulled out a rifle. Clutching it to her side, she said, "But next time, I'll be ready for them. Mark my words, that's the last time they'll get any of my hens."

"Mother! Put that rifle away," another woman called as she walked up from behind the house. "What are you doing? You know that's for predators only."

"These days you never know who will come to the door." Her mother huffed and stormed back into the house.

"I'm sorry," the younger woman said as she made her way to us. "My mother's getting more and more ornery every day. I hope she didn't scare you with that rifle."

"Not scare so much as put us a little on guard," Charlotte answered. "You just never know who's trigger happy and who isn't."

"Let me reassure you," the woman wearing gray cargo pants and a T-shirt said. "My mother hasn't used a firearm since the day my father took her to get licensed. He took her to the shooting range afterward as a sort of celebration. But that plan backfired," she added with a chuckle. "The weapon they were using had quite a kick to it. After one shot, mom landed on her backside, bruising her tailbone. She decided then and there that she didn't ever need to do that again. And that was that."

"Yet she keeps a rifle by the door?" I asked curiously. I understood wanting protection from the wildlife. They lived far enough into the country that they'd likely seen a bear or two before.

"I put it there after our chickens were raided," she said. "It's not that I'm going to go after the coyotes, or foxes, or maybe it's raccoons, but a warning shot would likely do the trick."

"That's understandable." I held out my hand and introduced Charlotte and myself.

"Marci Daze. It's nice to meet you, Marion." She nodded to my sister. "Charlotte."

I quickly filled her in on why we'd come to their farm. As I was explaining, a flock of unusual-looking chickens started appearing from around the house. They all had fancy plumes of feathers on their heads. There were a couple that reminded me of a phoenix with their orange-red coloring. But the most beautiful ones had black-and-white-speckled feathers that sort of mimicked a herringbone pattern.

"You want to know if this young woman Lacey was here?" she asked.

"Yes. Did she contact you about a job?"

"I did get a phone call," Marci said with a frown. "But honestly, I never called them back." She glanced around at the property, and sadness crept into her dark eyes. "It's obvious we need more help around here, but with Mom's medical bills, we just can't afford to hire anyone. We're barely keeping it together with the two guys helping with the pumpkin patch as it is."

"Did the woman who called leave a message?" I asked.

"She did, but I deleted it." She scrunched up her face. "Sorry. I wish I could be more help. I'm just so busy these days. I'm afraid I didn't even listen long enough to hear the woman's name. I heard she was looking for work and just deleted it."

"It's all right," I said, feeling deflated. It seemed as if Lacey had probably called, but I couldn't prove that without the recording. Not that it would make much of a difference other than to give us a time stamp as to when the call came in.

"Marci," Charlotte said, stepping up beside me.

"Yes?"

"Your mother was going on about wolves raiding the chickens. Do you think there's any validity to that?" Charlotte asked, making it sound like she was just vaguely curious.

"Wolves?" Marci looked taken aback. "We don't have wolves roaming around here, do we?" Before I could answer, realization dawned on the pretty woman's face. "Oh... She means the wolf shifters her new friend was telling her about." Marci *tsked*. "No. Mom met some woman at card night who put some crazy ideas in her head. I'd bet anything the animal that got our hens was a fox. I've seen one around here before. He's just been biding his time."

"Her new friend?" I asked. "Do you know her name?"

"Felicity, maybe?" Marci pursed her lips. "Francie?"

"Fiona?" I supplied.

"That's it! Fiona. She's also a farmer. Mom bonded with her over their love of the land. Do you know her?"

"We've met," I said dryly. It seemed impossible that so many people seemed to actually like the woman I'd met a few days ago, but I supposed anyone could have a bad day, right? Except most people were just frustrated when they were having a bad day. They didn't talk about wolf shifters as if they weren't even human. I had trouble believing that Fiona was as great as everyone said.

"Uh-oh," Marci said with a grimace. "Is she bad news? Should I keep Mom away from her?"

"That's a tough one," I said slowly, trying to gather my thoughts. "My interaction with her was less than pleasant, but she did seem a little stressed. She had a busted water line on her property, so I suppose that could make anyone short-tempered. But she was rather unpleasant to the two shifters who were there to help fix it. The entire thing left a bad taste in my mouth. But this morning my aunt told me she met Fiona at the card tournament and that both she and my dad had really enjoyed getting to know her."

"So you're saying that this Fiona is likely biased against wolf shifters?" Marci asked.

"It sure seemed like it after the way she treated Jax and Kai. And now she's putting stories in your mom's head about shifters raiding your chickens. It seems a little weird to me."

"Me, too," Marci said, her eyes full of steel. "I didn't love that this woman filled her head with the shifter stuff. Just because a man is a shifter that doesn't mean he's out raiding chickens for goodness' sake." Her tone was full of conviction, almost as if the attack felt personal. "But now, hearing about this, I'm sure Mom doesn't need to be hanging out with that lady. I don't care if she had rainbows flying out her ass. People always show their true colors."

"They really do, don't they?" Charlotte said, giving Marci a knowing smile.

Marci chuckled to herself. "I sound a little intense, don't I? It's just that I've seen firsthand what it does to a person when they are treated less than human, and I won't stand for it."

"Good for you," I said, admiring her strength of conviction.

"Listen, ladies, I have to get back to work. I'm sorry I couldn't be more helpful but thank you for the heads up on this Fiona woman. I'll talk to my mom and get her straightened out. Wolves. Of all the things." She shook her head and then turned to shoo the chickens ahead of her toward the back of the house.

Charlotte and I headed back to the SUV. Once we were strapped in and headed down the driveway, Charlotte said, "That was interesting."

"It was?" I glanced over at her before turning my attention back to the road.

"Sure. Fiona seems to be forming a white-hair posse."

"White-hair posse?" I parroted and then let out a bark of laughter. "Where'd that come from?"

"First Aunt Lucy and Dad, and now Marci's mother? All three of them seem to be enthralled by this Fiona lady. What's the one thing the three of them have in common?" she asked me.

"It's not white hair," I said with a laugh. "Aunt Lucy wouldn't be caught dead without her hair perfectly dyed."

Charlotte laughed. "True. But they are all of a certain age, actually seem to enjoy card tournaments"—she shuddered—"and they were hanging out at Hallucinations. *Hallucinations*, Marion. It's the perfect place to spike drinks."

"What are you saying, Charlotte? That Aunt Lucy, Dad, and Marci's mom have been cursed to like cranky old ladies who have some sort of grudge against wolf shifters?"

"Stranger things have happened," she said.

And I had to admit that she was right. Stranger things *had* happened and were likely to happen again. "Fine. Make a note that we should check on Lucy and Dad to make sure they aren't cursed or spelled to like Fiona."

"I already did." Charlotte turned her phone around and showed me her Notes app. "It's right after get a cooter wax."

"Cooter wax?" I asked with a snort.

"I booked you one, too. Tomorrow at eleven, since you can't seem to make the appointment on your own."

"You booked me a waxing appointment without even asking me?" I glanced over at her and scowled at her amused grin.

"I booked you for a cut and color, followed by a facial, and then an appointment for an allover body wax. When you get home, Jax is going to wonder who the goddess is that took over your body."

"You did what?" I gasped out, both a little horrified and grateful. It was true that I did need to get my hair done. And a facial sounded lovely. But a wax? "An *allover* body wax, Charlotte?"

She shrugged one shoulder. "I wasn't sure which bits you needed done, so I figured it was best to book for everything. You did say that since you turned fifty, hair is popping up in strange places. I was just trying to make sure you had all your bases covered."

My instinct was to groan. Instead, I just glanced over at her and said, "Thanks."

"You're welcome."

CHAPTER 14

*W*e spent the afternoon checking out the other farms in the area. Blueberries, Groveland Farms, and Happy Hollow. None of them had any record of Lacey Riley calling them or setting up an interview. The day was mostly a bust with the exception of the half-off sunflower bouquets we picked up from Happy Hollow. It was the end of their season, and they were desperately trying to move the last of their stock.

"We still need to go by Tazia's shop and Sky's the Limit," Charlotte said, eyeing our list.

"There's no time like the present," I said.

"Oh no." Charlotte shook her head violently. "First, you're going to feed me. I'm starving."

"I guess we can stop for a late lunch."

"We either stop, or you'll have to deal with hangry Charlotte. Your choice."

I sped up and said, "Late lunch it is."

"That's what I thought."

In less than five minutes, I pulled the SUV into the parking lot of Witches' Garden.

"Are you even allowed in there?" Charlotte asked, eyeing the restaurant that had almost burned down during one of my mixers.

"Ha. Ha. Bellatrix has completely forgiven me. Especially since I send a lot of first dates here."

"She's nicer than me," Charlotte quipped.

"A lot of people are nicer than you." The words just flew out of my mouth, and the second I heard them, I clasped my hand over my mouth.

My sister just looked at me and laughed. "No lies detected. Though you didn't have to be so blunt about it. Now come on. My stomach is trying to eat itself."

"Sorry," I muttered. "I didn't mean that."

She laughed. "Yes, you did. But you can make it up to me by buying lunch."

"Okay," I said and even managed to refrain from mentioning that I usually did when we were working.

The restaurant was lit with at least a thousand candles, and there were sage bundles in the middle of each table.

"You'd think after almost losing the place to fire once before that Bellatrix wouldn't ever light even one more candle," Charlotte observed after we were seated.

"They are spelled. The flame is an illusion," I said. Bellatrix had asked me if she could pay the coven to create the gorgeous aesthetic. I'd told her I'd ask, but no way was she paying for it. In the end, the coven had been happy to help. And with seven of us combining our power, it had only taken about ten minutes.

"You can't even tell," Charlotte said with awe in her voice.

"Marion!" Bellatrix called when she spotted us. "It's been a while since you've been in. How are you?"

"Doing pretty good. How's business?" I asked as I stood and gave her a hug.

"Booming. Know anyone looking for a job? We're short a few servers." She glanced past me and said hello to Charlotte.

"Only one," I said hesitantly. "But it's possible she's already come by or called you. Does the name Lacey Riley ring a bell?"

"Actually yes," she said, frowning and then giving a quick shake of her head. "But it appears your friend isn't all that interested in work. I told her I'd give her a try, but she never showed up."

I sucked in a sharp breath. It was our first solid lead. Not only that, but Bellatrix was someone I trusted. The information she gave us would be reliable. I just hoped there was something we could use to piece together Lacey's whereabouts on the day she disappeared. "Listen, Bellatrix, Lacey went missing yesterday. Charlotte and I are trying to trace her movements prior to her disappearance. Do you mind answering some questions?"

"She's missing?" Bellatrix clutched her crystal necklace, her eyes wide. "No wonder she didn't show up yesterday. She was supposed to come in around two to do paperwork and get a tour before she shadowed one of my other waitresses. Oh gosh. And here I was, angry and thinking uncharitable thoughts. Of course, I'll help in any way I can."

"Have a seat." I waved to the empty chair at our table as I

sat back down. Once Bellatrix was settled, I asked, "When did Lacey first come in?"

"Let me think." Bellatrix tapped the table with her fingers and said, "It was either Thursday or Friday."

"Anyway you can narrow that down?" I asked hopefully.

"Yeah, probably." She wrinkled her nose. "I swear, getting older sucks. The short-term memory is the first thing to go." Then she pulled out her phone, looked at her calendar, and said, "There. Demetri was the sous chef that day. I remember because he flirted with her when he brought me a new dish to try. So that was definitely Friday. Sometime between lunch and dinner. I'd say around three, probably."

"Friday. Okay," I said with a nod, unsure how that could help us if she went missing on Sunday. But it was a start. "Do you mind telling us about the interview?"

"There's not much to tell," Bellatrix said with a half shrug. "She was new in town. Looking to start over after the last place she worked went out of business. Said she moved here because her mother said it was her favorite place on earth. Decided if she needed to start over, she might as well do it in a 'magical place' as her mother had called it."

"Did her mother live here?" Charlotte asked, her expression hopeful.

"Oh, no." The restaurant owner shook her head. "Her mother came here on her honeymoon and then came back every anniversary up until her untimely death about twelve years ago." Bellatrix looked sad when she added, "Her dad didn't handle it well and married a woman half his age just three months later. They moved Back East, and Lacey said she hadn't heard from him since."

"She told you all that?" I asked. It wasn't something people usually talked about in an interview.

"You'd be surprised what people say when you give them space to talk about themselves," Bellatrix said. "If I've learned anything about interviewing potential staff after all these years, it's to listen more than speak. Usually they end up divulging something I never would have asked about. It gives me insight into who they are. With Lacey, I saw a young woman who just needed a break in life. That's why I was disappointed when she didn't show up yesterday."

I'd already known that Bellatrix was a good person, but her words just drove the point home.

"Did she say anything that might help us find her?" Charlotte asked. "Like where she lived, hours she was available, or if she'd interviewed with anyone else?"

"She said she was renting a studio apartment from an older couple here in Premonition Pointe. I assume a granny apartment or one over a garage." Bellatrix said. "But she didn't say where. She did say she was looking for a second job because she liked being outside and was hoping for something at a farm or nursery."

We already knew about her preference for a farm or nursery, but it was good to have confirmation. I just wished she'd given Bellatrix something more substantial that would give us a lead on her.

"The only other thing we talked about," Bellatrix continued, "was that she couldn't come in on Saturday because she was watching her neighbor's kid. They'd worked out an agreement to help each other out with childcare. The neighbor's name was Kelly, I think she said. Or was it Kelcy? I'm not sure. Something with a K."

"Kylie?" Charlotte asked, her brows raised. "Kylie Brickenson?"

"Kylie! That's it," Bellatrix exclaimed, beaming. "I knew it was a K name. I don't know about the last name, but it definitely was Kylie."

"Who's Kylie Brickenson?" I asked Charlotte.

"She's the woman I go to for my waxings at the Liminal Space Day Spa," she said excitedly. "Kylie has a little girl, about eight years old I think."

My heart started to pound. "Do you think she's working today?"

"I'm already on it." Charlotte had her phone out and was busy making the call.

I turned to Bellatrix. "Thank you so much for your help. If Kylie Brickenson really is her neighbor, this could be the break we need."

Bellatrix nodded once. Then she frowned at me. "Where are the PPPD in all this? Shouldn't they be handling this investigation?"

I let out a frustrated grunt. "You'd think so, but they have their sights set on Kai Gray with zero proof."

"Why would they do that? Was he seen with her or something?" Bellatrix asked.

"No. At least not the day she went missing. He did step in during an altercation with her ex on the beach the day before that, though. Jax and I were there. Kai was nothing but helpful. I think someone at the PPPD just has a thing against Kai and are looking to pin this on him with or without concrete proof."

"And you aren't going to stand for that," Bellatrix said

kindly. Then she reached over and squeezed my hand. "There should be more people like you in the world, Marion. Let me know if I can be of any more help."

"I will." I stood and gave her a hug.

"Marion, we have to go," Charlotte said, jumping out of her chair and grabbing her bag. "Kylie is with her last appointment right now. We gotta move if we want to catch her."

So much for that lunch, I thought, eyeing the empty table.

Charlotte grabbed my hand and hauled me after her. I glanced back and called, "Thanks again, Bellatrix."

"Give me your keys," Charlotte demanded when we got to the SUV.

"I can drive," I said, moving to open the driver's side door.

But once I had the door open, Charlotte bumped me out of the way and climbed in. "You're moving too slow. Get in. I've got this."

She started the vehicle and was already putting it in gear before I registered what was happening.

"I'll leave you here," she said.

Knowing she wasn't one to bluff, I hurried around to the other side and climbed in. Before I even got the door closed all the way, Charlotte stepped on the gas and whipped the SUV out of the parking lot.

"Holy shit, Char. You could have waited until I was strapped in at least."

"We don't have time." She floored it when the upcoming light turned yellow.

I grabbed the "oh shit" handle and held on. "I don't think

we need to risk our lives to catch her in time, do we? I mean, we know where to find her now."

Charlotte glanced over at me, her expression made of steel. "As far as we know, no one is actually looking for Lacey. If Kylie has some information, then maybe we'll get a clue about how to find her, right?"

"Well, sure…" I started.

"Then time is of the essence, right?" she demanded again.

"Yeah, I guess so."

"You guess so," she repeated. "If it were me or Ty or Jax, *you'd* be weaving in and out of this traffic right now."

My sister had a point. If one of my loved ones had disappeared, I'd do just about anything to find them. I gave my sister a long look. "You identify with Lacey, don't you?"

"What?" She took a turn a little too fast, making me slightly nauseated. "Why would you say that?"

"Because you're all in on trying to find her."

Charlotte didn't say anything at first, but then she finally responded. "I know what it feels like to think you're alone in the world. I can't stand the idea that Lacey must be feeling that now, wherever she is. So yeah. If we can help, then I'm going to do whatever I can."

"I'm with you," I said.

She smirked at me. "That's good, since I'm driving."

"Just get us there in one piece," I said.

When she pulled into the parking lot, I loosened my grip on the handle, more than ready to have my feet on solid ground.

Charlotte slowed, staking out a parking spot, but then

she suddenly pointed at a red Toyota Camry and said, "Oh no! There she goes!"

Before I could get a word out, Charlotte stepped on the gas and raced after the red car.

CHAPTER 15

"Whoa! What are you doing?" I cried.

"Following Kylie. What does it look like I'm doing?" Charlotte cut off a blue truck as she turned right out of the parking lot. The sound of horns blaring drowned out the song playing on the radio.

"You're going to get us into an accident," I said when the noise finally died down. "This is the last time I let you drive ever again."

"Don't get your panties in a wad," Charlotte said, speeding up to catch the red Toyota. "I've never been in an accident—"

"Yet," I said, cutting her off. "But if you keep this up, we might find ourselves at the bottom of that embankment."

"You're being dramatic." She swerved, passing a car that was going slower than she liked.

"Just don't kill us," I pleaded.

"I'll do my best."

My stomach rolled as she took a sharp turn and then sped up so that she was within two cars of Kylie's red Camry. When the one right in front of us stopped for a red light, Charlotte slammed on the horn and yelled out, "Move it, Grandpa!"

The older man in the white car in front of us put his hand out the window and flipped us off.

I kept my eyes glued to the red Camry. After the ride I'd had to endure, I'd be damned if we lost her now. "She's turning right," I told Charlotte, while pointing to the car as it disappeared.

My sister stepped on the gas, revving the engine as the light turned green and then cursing when the older man in front of us just sat there. She quickly swerved into the left turn lane and blew past him as she swerved back so we could go straight, all while giving him a taste of his own medicine as she waved her middle finger at him.

"We're going to get tossed in the slammer if the PPPD sees us," I said.

"Let them try and catch me." Charlotte turned right and sped down the street.

"Dammit!" I cried when I didn't see the red Camry. "We lost her."

"I'm not giving up just yet," she said as she swiveled her head, looking down each of the residential streets we passed. "She must live here somewhere. There's no way out of this neighborhood except the way we came in."

"How do you know that?" I asked her, frowning. Charlotte had only spent a handful of months in this town. She couldn't have a detailed understanding of each neighborhood as if she'd grown up in there.

"Denver and I might have been talking about getting a place together," she said flippantly.

"What?" I swiveled around so that I was staring at her. "When?"

"Don't get too excited," she said, rolling her eyes. "We don't have a plan. We've just been considering it and looking at what it would cost. No plans have actually been made."

"Oh." I briefly wondered what Minx would do if Charlotte moved out. The way the little dog had been acting ever since Jax had come home made me think that she might rebel if Charlotte made her leave her favorite person for even one night. Though it would free up some space on my bed.

Charlotte let out a frustrated huff. "That red Camry has to be here somewhere."

Knowing full well that if Kylie parked in a garage we were going to be SOL, I suggested we systematically drive down each street until we found the Camry in question.

"Yeah, that should work. I hope," Charlotte agreed.

For the next twenty minutes, we rolled by each house as if we were casing the joints, and when we got to the last street on the road, my stomach started to ache with anxiety. If we didn't find Kylie, that was just one more day away from any possibility of finding Lacey.

"I don't see it— Wait! Look over there!" Charlotte pointed to a silver Airstream trailer. Just behind it was a flash of red. "That has to be it."

Please don't let it be some other red car, I silently begged.

Charlotte swung around and parked behind the Camry,

pulling in so close it would be impossible to get the car out as long as the trailer was still there.

"Was that necessary?" I asked her when the two bumpers gently tapped.

"I didn't want her to flee."

"Why would she do that? It's not like we're here to haul her off to jail. We just want some information about her neighbor."

"You never know, Marion," Charlotte said, exasperation in her tone. "It doesn't hurt to be prepared."

I guess she had me there. We climbed out of my SUV and then stood on the street, staring at the houses. "Which one do you think it is?" I asked her.

"It's not that one." Charlotte pointed to the sunny yellow house on the left.

"Why?"

"There's no car in the driveway. If Kylie lived there, she probably wouldn't park on the street," she said with an air of arrogance.

"Maybe. Unless she shares a house with someone and they park there," I reasoned.

"There's plenty of room for two cars there. No. Not the yellow house. Not the forest green one either. See that garage apartment? I bet that's where Lacey was living. I'm going with the sea blue cottage with the bike on the front lawn."

I had to admit that her logic was sound. "Okay, let's give it a go." With Charlotte on my heels, I followed the stone steps up to the small white porch and knocked. I heard the voice of a child yelling for their mom followed by the door opening.

"Can I help you?" the young woman who couldn't have been a day over twenty-five asked, looking pensive.

"Kylie!" Charlotte said, pushing me out of the way. "Thank goodness. I thought for sure we'd lost you."

"Charlotte? What are you doing here? And what do you mean you thought you'd lost me?" she asked, raising one eyebrow.

"Oh, that. We were trying to catch you as you were leaving work, but you were already in your car, headed home. So we followed you," Charlotte explained as if it didn't sound crazy that we'd tailed her back to her house.

"You followed me home? What is this, some sort of waxing emergency?"

I couldn't help but notice the pointed look Kylie gave me while she said, 'waxing emergency.'"

Charlotte chuckled as she eyed me. "It is, but that's not why we're here."

I cleared my throat. "I am really sorry to bother you at home, Ms. Brickenson. Normally we do not barge in on our beauty professional's private lives. But this is important. We're here about Lacey Riley."

"Have they found her yet?" Kylie looked past me and scanned the area, her gaze finally landing on the garage apartment next door. Charlotte had definitely gotten that part right. "She's not... not—" Kylie held her hand to her mouth as her eyes welled with tears. "Tell me she's okay. Please."

I shared a quick glance with my sister. Then I frowned. "I'm sorry, but no. There's no indication that they've found her yet. And that's why we're here."

Tears overflowed Kylie's eyes, and she hastily wiped them away. "I'm so worried about her."

"We are too," Charlotte chimed in. "Do you mind if we ask some questions? We're trying to trace Lacey's steps the day she disappeared."

"Do you work with the police or something?" Kylie asked, sniffling.

"No," I said, wondering what I should tell her. If she thought I was only here to clear someone's name, surely she'd slam the door in our faces. "I met Lacey down on the beach the day before she went missing."

"The day her ex showed up?" Kylie volunteered.

"Yes. And ever since then, I've been worried. And after I learned she went missing, I just can't shake the feeling that the PPPD isn't dedicating enough resources to looking for her. So my sister and I thought we'd check around town to see if we can piece together what she was doing and who she might have seen. If nothing else, we can give the information to the detectives."

Kylie sucked in a sharp breath and then scowled as she said, "That won't help. The officers I spoke to aren't interested in answers. All they seem to care about is their own narrative."

"To be honest, I've been suspecting the same thing. It's why we're out here trying to find out what really happened," I said.

"And when you do... then what?" she asked, sounding suspicious. "Do you think you'll get them to listen?"

I shook my head. "No. But we have contacts with law enforcement outside of Premonition Pointe. The type of departments that can overrule the local police force," I explained, hoping that was true. The Magical Task Force certainly could and did overrule them on a regular basis, but unless Lacey had magic, I wasn't sure they could do anything. Though if the PPPD kept focusing on the wolves and they were innocent, the MTF probably would step in. "If we can find evidence that can lead us to Lacey, I think they can help."

Relief washed over Kylie's face. "Oh my gosh. Do you really have someone who can help? I told Officer Stone that John was here the day she disappeared and—"

"John, her ex?" I gasped out. "The one who had a restraining order against him?"

Charlotte placed her hand on my arm, and instantly Kylie's aura appeared around her. The outer layer was a muddied red color, indicating stress, but the inside, closest to her body, was a vibrant, deep blue, and I knew in that moment that Kylie was telling the truth.

"Yes. He came by her apartment yesterday morning. I saw them out by the stairs talking. When I told the officer that, he wrote it down but didn't ask any questions about the interaction or anything. He acted like it wasn't important at all. He just kept asking if I knew what she had planned that day."

My mind whirled. Why wasn't John the primary suspect? He'd been seen with Lacey that day. He hadn't been out of town, or at the very least he'd come *back* to town, and the police didn't seem to be concerned? Something was seriously off. "That's almost unbelievable," I said, trying to keep my temper in check. "But I know you're telling the truth."

"You do? How?"

"Charlotte and I can see auras," I admitted. "Do you have any idea why Stone wasn't interested in John's presence? Did they know each other or something?"

"I have no idea." Kylie chewed on her bottom lip. "Lacey hasn't lived here long. And she certainly never lived here with John, so I don't know how the officer would have known him. It just doesn't make sense to me."

Me neither. "That is very strange," I agreed. "Did you tell Stone anything else?"

"Just that Lacey had a job interview that afternoon. I was watching Cody. She was supposed to call me when the interview was over and before she started her shift at the Witches' Garden. I never heard from her and when she didn't show back up here that night, I called the police, knowing something was wrong. She'd never just leave Cody like that."

"Interview?" Charlotte asked. "Do you know where?"

"She didn't say the name, just that she was headed to a place out on Pointe Meadow. The job was temporary harvesting with the possibility of full-time off-season work in the barn."

"Pointe Meadow?" I repeated, my entire body going cold. "You're sure that's where she was headed?"

"I'm sure. There's a house at the end that I've been in love with since I was a kid. A big white farmhouse with a wraparound porch and a large sunroom on the west side. I remember telling her to swing by and take a look at it. This time of year, it's always decorated with elaborate Halloween decorations." Kylie sniffed. "I don't think she ever made it to that house."

"You think she went missing before that?" Charlotte

asked, and I was grateful she was still putting the puzzle pieces together, because I was stuck on Pointe Meadow.

The Gray Wolf Winery was on Pointe Meadow. And suddenly I knew exactly why Stone was so gung-ho to blame this all on Kai.

"Yes. Her car was found on the side of the road with a flat tire about a mile from Pointe Meadow. I think she got a flat, went for help, and that's when she went missing."

"Who did you hear that from?" I asked, knowing the PPPD wasn't going to be forthcoming with any information, especially to Lacey's neighbor.

"My brother-in-law works for the wrecker company that towed her car." Kylie glanced around as if looking to see if anyone was paying attention to them. Then she continued. "He told me this morning that the PPPD hasn't even come to search her car yet."

"Oh boy," Charlotte said, almost to herself.

"Can you believe that? It's like they aren't even looking for her." There were tears in Kylie's eyes. "I'm so worried, but I don't have a clue what I can even do."

I reached out and squeezed her hand. "Kylie, you might not realize it yet, but you have just given us a treasure trove of information that we can look into. Before we found you, we were also spinning our wheels, but now we can really dig in and see if we can find Lacey and get her home. Thank you."

"I really hope so," she said earnestly. Then she glanced at the garage apartment next door. "Will you keep me updated?"

"You'll be the first to know if we find anything," I promised her. It was the least I could do after all the information she'd supplied. "Is there anything else you can think of that we should know?"

Kylie thought for a moment and then shook her head. "I can't think of anything, but if you have more questions, please don't hesitate to ask."

"That's kind of you." After we exchanged numbers, we thanked her again and then retreated to my SUV.

CHAPTER 16

"Where to first?" Charlotte asked as she headed for the driver's side of my SUV.

"Oh no. Your driving days are over," I said, pushing her out of the way. "You're lucky I didn't lose my cookies after that speed demon display."

Charlotte rolled her eyes. "Fine. Stop being so dramatic."

We climbed into the vehicle, and I hesitated for a moment, not sure what to do first.

"Well, Marion?" Charlotte demanded, impatient for the plan.

"I'm thinking. What I really want to do is head to the police department and give them a piece of my mind. Find out why they aren't looking into John."

"Then let's go," she said. "We'll talk to the police chief. That way if anything hinky is going on with Stone and his partner, someone from the top can look into it."

"Let me just call Brix first. He said he'd put out some feelers." I grabbed my phone and hit Call. It went straight to voice mail. I groaned. "He's out of pocket. Okay. We'll head to the station and see what we can find out."

Ten minutes later, we were walking out of the police station with zero progress. The chief wasn't there. They'd offered to let us speak to a beat cop, but I'd declined. It just didn't feel right to talk to anyone except the chief.

"We'll come back tomorrow," Charlotte said.

"Yeah," I said, feeling frustrated. We'd finally gotten a break in the case, and I wasn't sure what to do with it. I led the way around the corner to my SUV. We'd parked on the side street, hoping not to draw attention to the fact that we were at the police station. Just as we were about to reach my vehicle, Charlotte nudged me.

"Look," Charlotte said, her voice low.

I followed her gaze to the lot behind the station and spotted Stone and Wallis standing near their patrol car. Stone was looking away from us, toward the busier street, while Wallis leaned down, talking to someone in a gray Nissan four-door sedan. A scowl claimed my lips, and I started to dismiss them until Wallis pulled out a thick wad of cash, handed it to the driver, and then took a brown paper bag in return.

Warning bells went off in my head. Did I just see what I thought I saw? Were Stone and Wallis buying drugs? Was that why it looked like Stone was trying to shield Wallis from view? There was no way to know what was in that paper bag, but it didn't look like a food delivery. The bag was far too small.

Wallis suddenly glanced over at us and said something to Stone.

Stone turned around, scowled, and then hurried toward

us. I debated just getting in the SUV and leaving. It's not like we were breaking the law. But I decided I wanted to hear what Stone had to say.

"What can I do for you, Mr. Stone?" I said, my tone icy.

"You can keep your nose out of everyone's business," he practically growled.

"I'm sorry?" I asked, playing dumb.

"Don't think we don't know that you're nosing around, trying to interfere in our case. Do you have any idea what kind of trouble you've caused by having that sniveling idiot from the MTF call here?"

I wanted to pump my fist in the air, knowing that Brix had ruffled some feathers, but I kept my cool. "I don't know what you're talking about."

"Yes you do. If you know what's good for you, you'll go back to your little matchmaking business and keep your nose out of police affairs."

"If you did your job," I said sweetly. "I wouldn't have to interfere, now would I?"

I heard Charlotte suck in a breath. Maybe I shouldn't have said that, but the officer was baiting me, and sometimes a girl just snapped.

His expression turned stony. "Stay. Out. Of. It. Or else it's you who's going to pay the price. Understand?"

"Are you threatening me, *Officer Stone?*"

"I'd take it that way if I were you." He turned and started to leave but then paused and added, "I'm sure you wouldn't want us to arrest your guard dog, would you?"

I WAS STILL FUMING when we got back to the office. How dare Stone threaten Jax? I was going to take him down if it was the last thing I did.

"Marion, calm down," Charlotte said, leaning on her desk and munching the fries we'd picked up from the local burger joint on the way back. "I think there's actually steam coming out of your ears."

"I wouldn't doubt it," I said through clenched teeth, staring at my uneaten lunch. "I don't think I've been this mad since that time you washed my favorite white dress with your red jeans and turned it bubble gum pink."

"That *is* mad," she said and held her hands in the air as if I was going to attack her.

I couldn't even bring myself to laugh. Instead, I picked up the phone and called Sebastian. After relaying what we'd learned from Kylie, he said, "Do you want me to put a PI on John?"

"Yes," I agreed instantly. "Do you have the information on his background check yet?"

"We have the record of the restraining order that Lacey filed against him, but there is no work history or even a stable address for him. It appears the man has always worked under the table, assuming he worked, and has never owned a home or even rented one in his name. The address he has on file is his grandmother's, and that house is empty and has been condemned according to county records."

"That's gonna make it hard for a PI to find him, isn't it?" I said, sitting back in my chair and covering my eyes with my other hand.

"Maybe, but don't worry, Marion. We'll find information

on him. We always do. And the PI can trace things in a way that we can't. I'll call as soon as I know anything."

"What about Lacey's background check?"

"Looks like she's been on her own since she was fifteen. Was in legal trouble once when she was stealing food at age sixteen. Since then, her record is clean. Her last known address was down in Fresno. That's where I'm sending the PI to dig up information on John."

"Okay. Thanks, Sebastian."

"Sure thing."

"Nothing?" Charlotte asked.

"Nothing useful." I drummed my fingers on the desk and then finally tapped my computer and opened my search engine. I typed in Gray Wolf Winery and Help Wanted.

The second return on my search was for an online ad posting for seasonal harvest workers for Gray Wolf Winery.

"Oh man," I muttered to myself and picked up my phone again to call Kai.

"Marion," he said when he answered. "What can I do for you?"

"Hey, Kai. I just learned you guys are hiring seasonal help out there at the winery."

He chuckled. "Are you looking for a part-time job? We can always use some help picking the grapes and tending the fields."

"Ha, no. Not yet, but if business stays in the toilet, you never know," I quipped. "Actually, I'm trying to find out if you had any interviews lined up this week."

"Why?" he asked, suddenly sounding suspicious.

I hadn't wanted to directly ask him about Lacey, preferring instead that he just tell me if he'd had a meeting with her on the books. But it was obvious from his tone that he wasn't going to do that. I cleared my throat. "Well, as it turns out, we learned that Lacey was on her way to a job interview when she went missing. An interview out on Pointe Meadow. Since I saw your online ad, I was wondering—"

"You think she was coming here and that I or the pack abducted her?" His tone was full of venom. "Really, Marion? That's what you think of me?"

"Um, no? I'm just trying to follow all the leads and cross you and the pack off the list." I hadn't actually thought that, but now I was wondering. Why was he so defensive?

"Right. I'm sure that's exactly what you're doing. For your information, no, I did not have any interviews set up. But if I'd known that woman was looking for work, I'd have hired her just to give her a break. I have to go." The line went dead, and I stared at the phone for a long moment, wondering what just happened.

"That doesn't sound like it went well," Charlotte said.

I glanced up at her. "No. It didn't. Not at all."

"Looks like I might need to find a new date for Autumn then," she said as she tapped on her computer.

I just nodded, wondering if I'd been wrong about Kai and the pack all along. His reaction had been way over the top. I understood being frustrated when everyone suspected you of wrongdoing just because of who and what you were, but I hadn't accused him of anything. Had I?

Maybe deep down I had.

An ache formed in the pit of my stomach as I tossed my lunch in the trash, knowing I wasn't going to be able to eat.

CHAPTER 17

"*M*arion!" Autumn called as she rushed to catch up with me.

I stopped at the entrance to the trail that led to the bluff where we were meeting the coven and waited for the pottery shop owner.

"Hey," she said, smiling brightly. "It's a gorgeous evening, isn't it?"

I glanced up, realizing that I hadn't even noticed. The moon was full and there was only a slight chill in the air. "Yeah, it is. Good night for a cleansing ritual."

"It's my first one. So I'm excited." She slipped her arm through mine, and we made our way along the trail. "Tell me about Kai. Have you made any plans for our first date yet?"

I held back a wince. "Not yet. He's been kind of busy. But Charlotte is working on finding some men for a mixer if you're up for it."

"Oh," she said, looking disappointed. But then she

quickly brightened. "Sure. I guess it doesn't hurt to give it a go, right? No sense in putting all my eggs in one basket."

"Definitely," I said, feeling defeated. I already knew Kai was her match, but after yesterday's phone call, I just wasn't sure if he was going to talk to me again. And if there was any suspicion of Kai or the pack being involved in Lacey's disappearance, Kai was a nonstarter.

Again, my stomach started to ache at the idea that Kai was involved. It made me feel... wrong. Like I was totally on the wrong track. I put those thoughts aside and tried to clear my mind so I was ready for the cleansing.

"Hey! You made it," Grace said, running over to give both me and Autumn a hug when we reached the circle. All of the other coven members were already there and had prepped the circle with salt and white pillar candles.

"Are we late?" I asked Grace as I glanced around.

"Oh no." She shook her head. "I was just so eager to lose this energy that I came early to get it all set up."

"Then let's get to it," Hope said, clapping her hands together. Then she waved Grace into the middle of the circle as the rest of us took our places on the edge around her. When Autumn stood back, Carly waved for her to stand next to her.

"Sorry," Autumn said. "I've never done this before. I wasn't sure what to do."

"Just stand there behind the candle and follow along," Carly said. Then she glanced around. "Who's leading this shindig?"

"I am," Hope said as she raised her hand.

I glanced around, noting that in addition to Hope, Grace, and Carly, the rest of the coven, Iris, Gigi, and Joy, were there, too. It had been a while since we'd all been together, and the collective energy began to make me feel better.

"Let the cleansing begin!" Hope cried and raised her arms. Instantly, flames ignited on the candles as they rose in the air seemingly all on their own. It was a ritual I was completely familiar with as all of our callings and spells started the same way.

Magic encircled the coven, making me feel like an important part of the small group we'd formed. Each of us tapped into each other, giving and receiving our powers for the greater good. Participating in the coven rituals always made me feel more grounded. More connected. Like I had a purpose.

We chanted along with Hope and watched as magic poured into Grace. The energy around Grace turned into a dark fog, becoming jet black the longer our magic penetrated her.

Our chants were being drowned out by the wind, and the flames on the candles had enlarged, flickering angrily as the rancid energy clung to Grace.

"Goddess of above, speak the name of the cursed one who tainted Grace's energy and release her from their hold!" Hope called.

We all repeated the chant over and over until finally the wind whistled and then vanished altogether.

We all stood there, staring at the darkness clinging to Grace.

I was certain the spell hadn't worked and worried that she'd be tainted with the sour energy for the foreseeable future. But then the wind whipped up again, and with it, a voice spoke the name, "Sharon Krass."

The black energy clinging to Grace shattered into a million pieces, and our coven mate fell to her knees, exhausted.

"Finally," Hope said, letting out a huge sigh.

There were murmurs among the members, all expressing their relief.

Autumn started to take a step back, but Carly grabbed her wrist and said, "Not yet. There's still more to do before we close the spell."

Grace looked up at Carly, appearing confused, but then she closed her eyes and nodded. She grabbed the white tote bag near her feet and pulled out a green journal. As she got to her feet, she held it out in front of her and said, "Now."

Hope started to chant again. This time it was a burning spell. We all repeated her chants until the journal flew from Grace's hands and went up in flames, the smoke appearing bright white.

The moment the book vanished, the smoke swirled around Grace and folded in on itself, and when the chaos stopped, the smoke had formed an image.

An image of a man.

The man looked exactly like John Vincent. Lacey's ex.

The man I'd met on the beach.

I let out a sharp gasp.

"You know him?" Hope asked me.

I nodded. "He's the man I think abducted Lacey."

Everyone started talking at once.

I sank to the ground, my head spinning. There were clues everywhere, but I couldn't make much sense of them. What did John have to do with Grace's journal?

"What I don't understand," Grace said, cutting through

the chatter, "is why this John guy appeared when I was burning the energy of Sharon."

I jerked my head up. "What?"

Grace blinked at me. "The journal was all the dark thoughts I've been having ever since my energy was tainted. The energy that came from Sharon Krass." Grace made a face. "I should have known she was the cause. That woman was the absolute worst. You know, the type that acts sweet but is really a snake in the grass. Real backstabber energy. Anyway, when her lowball offer was rejected, she blamed me and then send me a lawyer letter, terminating our agreement while asking to be reimbursed for her time."

"You're kidding. She wanted you to pay her?" Hope asked.

Grace nodded. "But there's no contract or precedent for that, so I had Sebastian send her a letter back saying if she wanted payment for anything, she'd have to sue for it. I haven't heard anything since. Now I'm guessing she cursed me instead. Rude bitch."

"Who is Sharon?" I asked, still trying to make heads or tails of what had just happened.

"Who is she?" Grace parroted. "Oh, she's just a woman who walked into my office about a month ago and said she wanted to look for a house. I honestly don't know much about her. She had cash and bank statements to prove it."

"So we don't know how she's connected to John?" I asked. "Or anybody else for that matter?"

"No. All I know is that she's not married and she lives at the base of the mountain. All of that was on the offer paperwork," Grace said. "But don't tell anyone I said that. It's a breach of privacy that really could get me in trouble."

"Right." I stood, glanced around at my coven mates, and said, "Looks like I need to call Sebastian again. These background checks are starting to add up."

Gigi walked over and gave me a hug. "He'll get you the answers you need."

I nodded. "He always does. Thank him for me, will you?"

She nodded. "Of course."

I turned and headed for the trailhead.

"Marion!" Grace called.

"Yeah?" I said as I paused and glanced back.

"Let us know if we can help, okay?"

"Always." Then I hurried back to my vehicle, and on my way home, I called Sebastian.

When I walked in my house, the place was dead silent. Minx wasn't even there to greet me. I pulled out my phone to call Jax but then saw the text on my home screen.

Jax: *Going out tonight for a run. See you tomorrow morning.*

I glanced out the window at the full moon and headed straight for the freezer. It was definitely going to be an ice cream-for-dinner night.

CHAPTER 18

*R*inging woke me from a fitful sleep. I rolled over and grabbed the phone and then sat up in bed when I noted Brix's name on the screen. "Brix," I said, sleep still in my gravelly voice. "What do you have for me?"

"I'm sorry. Did I wake you?" he asked.

"Yeah, but no matter. Did you find anything out about the PPPD?"

From the corner of my eye, I spotted Jax stretching. When I glanced at him, I saw that his torso was naked and he had a few fresh scratches on his chest. Apparently his run under the full moon had included a trip through the woods.

"Yeah," he said, his tone suddenly harsh. "Listen, Marion, I have some bad news."

I stiffened and averted my gaze from Jax's bare ass as he rose and headed to the bathroom. "What is it?"

"I don't think the PPPD is prejudiced against wolves. At least not systemically. The chief didn't give me that impression, and he said he hasn't had any problems with that in the past."

"Oookay. If that's the case, then why are they going so hard after Kai and the pack? If there's no evidence—"

"There *is* evidence. They found wolf tracks near Lacey's car where it was abandoned."

"Of course they did," I said with a scoff. "Kai's pack lives about a mile from there. It makes perfect sense that they'd find tracks in that area. That doesn't mean they had anything to do with her disappearance."

"True," Brix said. "However, there were human footprints along with the wolf tracks that went right up to the driver's side door. Like it or not, that makes any wolves in the area suspects. Including Jax."

"But Jax has an alibi!" I cried and then grimaced as Jax appeared in the bathroom door, a toothbrush in his mouth. He was staring at me with tired eyes and a wary expression on his face.

"I know that, and he's not on my list of suspects, but it does explain why the PPPD questioned him."

"*Your* list of suspects?" I asked Brix.

"Yes, mine. If wolves are involved, this is a Magical Task Force case. They should have brought it to us immediately. When I told the chief at the police department that, he got defensive and said he knows how to protect his residents and doesn't need some 'magical cowboy coming in like a bull in a China shop' and acting like they're the only one who can solve crimes. He said wolves aren't black magic users or demons, and they can handle it."

"And what did you say?" I asked my boss.

"I told him it wasn't his call and that I was taking the case away from him. It's now ours."

"Ours?" My heart started to beat rapidly. If Brix was bringing me in on the case, they'd have to give me access to their notes and interviews.

"Yes. Ours. I'm putting you and Charlotte on it until I can get there. I'm still wrapping up this case with the demon in Northern Idaho. I'll send you the files so you can get caught up, and I'll call when I'm on the way."

I sat frozen for a minute, unable to believe this stroke of luck. Now there wouldn't be anything hindering me from looking at every angle when it came to Lacey's case. "When can I expect the files?"

"Check your email. They should be there now. Listen, Marion, I've got to get going. You and Charlotte be careful. If a wolf really did this and they are connected to a pack, you could be walking into a shitstorm. Carry that dagger with you everywhere you go. Understand?"

"Got it." I ended the call and looked up at Jax. "It looks like a wolf really did take Lacey."

"That's bullshit," he said as he walked back into the bathroom.

I slipped out of bed and put my robe on as I made my way to the open bathroom door. Leaning against the frame, I crossed my arms over my chest and stared at him. "How do you know it's bullshit?"

"Because the only wolves around here are me, Trish, and Kai and the pack. None of us took Lacey. That's absurd." He spit out his toothpaste and rinsed his mouth with water.

"But how do you know it wasn't one of the pack? Or even Trish for that matter?" I didn't believe for a second

Trish would do such a thing, but I'd learned long ago that making assumptions when it came to what people were capable of was a fool's errand.

"You can't be serious." Jax pulled a T-shirt over his head and then glared at me. "Are you accusing them just because they are shifters, Marion?"

"No," I said with a heavy sigh. "I'm trying to rule everyone out so that I can concentrate on who actually did this. If I find evidence of some other wolf in town, then I'll follow that lead, too. You know I'm not accusing anyone just because of their wolf status. I'm narrowing down the field. Geez, Jax. I'm not some bigot. You know better than that."

"I thought I did," he said coolly and then brushed past me.

He shoved his feet into his shoes, grabbed his keys off the dresser, and stormed out.

"Where are you going?" I called after him.

But he didn't answer.

I flopped down on the couch and didn't even notice when my sister walked out of her bedroom.

"Rough morning?" she asked.

I startled and then looked up at her. She had Minx in her arms, and her hair resembled an impressive bird's nest.

"Sorry we woke you up. I didn't even know you were here," I said.

"Minx and I got home pretty late. Denver had to work early, and I wanted to sleep in." She sat down beside me. "Want to fill me in on what happened?"

"Brix called," I said with a sigh. "We're now officially on Lacey's case."

"And that's a problem because…"

"It looks like at least one of our suspects is a wolf, and Jax is angry that I have to consider Kai and the pack." I quickly ran through what Brix told me on the phone and filled in the details of my fight with Jax.

"That's unfortunate," Charlotte said. Then she frowned. "You know, looking at it from this angle, I guess I can see why the PPPD was going so hard on Kai. He does seem like the obvious suspect, right?"

"Yes," I agreed reluctantly. "Especially after he got so defensive Monday when I asked if Lacey had an interview scheduled."

"No more defensive than Jax just got, and you don't think he took her, do you?" Charlotte asked.

I met my sister's gaze and let out a small chuckle. "That was uncalled for."

"I'm just stating facts. Listen, I agree we have to keep him as a person of interest, but until there is more than circumstantial evidence, then he's not really a suspect, is he?"

"No. He isn't." I stood. "I'm getting coffee. Want some?"

"That's like asking if I want chocolate. Duh. Is the answer ever no?"

Ten minutes later, with coffee and a couple of bagels, Charlotte and I sat at my kitchen table with my laptop and Brix's files open. There wasn't much to go on. All it had was the interviews Stone and Wallis had conducted. Notably, the record of the conversation with Kylie was missing any mention of John. But everything else was what we suspected. Jax had an alibi. Kai said he was at the winery all day with the pack. There was camera footage showing his various pack members on the property, but none of Kai. He said that was because he was in his house and didn't have the cameras pointing inside. But it did show him coming out when Jax and his foreman arrived.

"This is mostly useless," Charlotte said as she clicked out.

"I agree. They seem to think that Kai found a way in and out of his house that the cameras didn't record. That's it. The tracks around the car and that flimsy theory," I said.

"But he could still be a suspect," Charlotte said, though she looked skeptical. "I suppose it's possible Kai could have slipped out as a wolf."

"No way!" Celia popped in, appearing in the chair across from me. "Kai Gray is no more the abductor than I am. Do you remember me telling you how boring he is? I'd bet my life on his innocence. No one who is that dull and practical is hauling women away and leaving a car with any sort of evidence behind."

"Bet your life?" Charlotte asked, amused. "You're already dead."

Celia waved an unconcerned hand. "You know what I mean. Kai is the type of meticulous wolf that just wouldn't be so sloppy. Besides, he's not the only wolf in town. I think you two need to start looking at other suspects."

Before I could say another word, my bubbly ghost vanished again.

Charlotte looked at me. "I think she has a point."

"Who does that leave? Kai's pack mates, but they are all accounted for on the video footage." I forced myself to add the next part, even though it hurt in my soul to say the words. "And then there's Jax." I grimaced and quickly said, "But he has a really good alibi, too."

"What about Trish? She's a wolf," Charlotte said.

"You think Trish has something to do with this?" I asked, my eyes wide. It wasn't something I wanted to believe, but if I'd learned one thing while working for the Magical Task Force it was that anything was possible.

"If you're questioning Kai and Jax, why aren't you questioning her?" Charlotte asked logically.

She had a point. I got out my phone and called her. "Trish? Do you have some time today?"

CHAPTER 19

After I showered and dressed, I walked into the kitchen and started pulling items out of the refrigerator. "Are you interested in a real breakfast? Egg burritos?"

"I'm in," Charlotte said as she sipped from her coffee mug.

I glanced at the machine, pleased to see she'd made a full pot. After I poured myself another mug, I said, "I think we need to regroup and figure out what we know and what we don't know about Lacey's disappearance."

My sister tapped her legal pad with her pen and said, "I'm way ahead of you."

I raised a curious eyebrow. "You are? What have you got?"

She tucked her red locks behind her ear and lifted the pad as she read off her list. "John, her ex, was seen at her place the morning Lacey went missing. The last place she was presumed to be was in her car about a mile from Pointe

Meadow. There is evidence a wolf and someone in human form were at the scene when or just after Lacey got her flat tire. Her car has been towed, but according to the records we got from the PPPD, no one has searched it. That's pretty much it."

I stirred the eggs in the pan and said, "Do we think it's possible that John is a shifter?"

"If he is, it would certainly make a lot more sense that he's the wolf who abducted Lacey rather than Kai or the pack," Charlotte reasoned.

"If he's a wolf, then I don't understand why the PPPD hasn't investigated him more," I said. "And why didn't they search Lacey's car for clues?"

Charlotte pursed her lips. "Maybe they're covering for John for some reason."

"But they did arrest him after he was harassing Lacey."

"You're right, it doesn't make any sense." Charlotte tapped her pen again. "Maybe we just need to face facts. Sometimes the answer really is the most obvious one."

"That they're egotistical assholes who are just bad at their jobs?" I sprinkled some shredded cheese into the eggs and stirred.

"Exactly." My sister raised her mug up in a mock toast.

Once the eggs were done, I fixed up the burritos and brought our plates to the table. "What have we decided on?"

"I think we need to find out if John is a shifter." She took a bite of her burrito and let out a moan of pleasure. "Oh my gosh. I had no idea how starving I was. Thank you for this."

Minx came running over and jumped on Charlotte's leg. She looked down at her. "People eat first, baby. Mama will get you some bites after we're done." The little dog continued to paw at her leg.

I laughed. "She thinks she *is* people."

Charlotte rolled her eyes as I got up and scraped the tiny bit of egg left in the pan onto a small paper plate and then put it on the floor for her. Minx went to town on the nibbles while Charlotte frowned at me. "You're spoiling her."

"Ha! That little dog arrived at this house spoiled," I countered.

"Maybe, but we're working on her manners, and now she'll never leave me alone while I'm eating."

I just shrugged and then grinned at her.

"You need to call Jax," Charlotte said, changing the subject.

"Jax? Why?" With the way he'd stormed off earlier, I highly doubted he was interested in hearing from me anytime soon.

"To find out if he thinks John is a shifter."

"Wouldn't he have told me that after we first met him?" I had trouble believing that if Jax thought John was a wolf that he wouldn't have filled me in.

"Probably, but we should still ask to cover our bases," she said logically.

I stifled a groan and picked up my phone. She was right, of course. But why did she think of this immediately after we'd argued? It was time to rip the bandage off. I hit Jax's name on my phone and waited.

The line rang three times, and I honestly thought he was going to send me to voice mail, but on the fourth ring, he picked up. "Yeah?"

It wasn't the most affectionate greeting, but I'd take it. "Hi. Charlotte and I are brainstorming the case this morning—"

He let out an irritated snort, which I ignored.

"And we're thinking the most logical suspect is John."

He didn't respond.

I barreled on. "We were wondering if there's a chance that John might be a shifter. Is that something you guys just know when you meet someone, or do you have to find out like everyone else does?"

There was nothing but more silence.

"Jax?" I hadn't thought it was that hard of a question.

"I'm here. I was thinking back to when I first met the pack after I'd been turned, and to be honest, I do think I felt some sort of kinship with them, but I didn't know what it was then. I don't remember feeling anything like that with John, but then I'm sure my senses were clouded since he was manhandling Lacey."

"Does that mean you don't know?" I asked.

"That means I don't know. If pressed, I'd say it's unlikely, but I'm not 100% certain. You should ask Kai. He might have a better feel for those things."

"Okay. I will."

"Is that all?" he asked, sounding impatient.

Was I supposed to say anything else? Was he waiting for me to apologize? Did I have anything to apologize for? I didn't think so. It wasn't as if I'd been accusing him of anything. Still, he'd obviously been upset, so I said, "I'm sorry about our disagreement this morning."

He sighed and then just said, "Me, too. Look, Marion, I've got to get back to work. We can talk tonight, okay?"

"Okay," I said, but he'd already ended the call before I even got the word out.

"Everything better between you two?" Charlotte asked.

"Doesn't quite seem like it, but I'm sure this will blow over. He told me to call Kai and ask about John being a shifter. Jax said he just wasn't sure."

"Then I guess you better get to callin'." She took another bite of her burrito.

I did as she said and got a cool-sounding Kai on the other end of the line.

"Yes, I can tell," Kai said. "And no, John wasn't a shifter."

Disappointment washed over me, and I mentally cursed the universe for making my life just a little harder. "Thank you, Kai. I really appreciate it. If you hear of any other shifters in the area, can you let me know?"

"Why would I do that?"

I could see this wasn't going to go anywhere productive, but I had to be honest with him. "There is reason to believe Lacey encountered a wolf before she disappeared. All I'm trying to do is track down who that might have been so I can ask some questions. I can't leave any stone unturned."

"Just ask questions. Sure." The skepticism was dripping from his tone.

I supposed I couldn't blame him. If I'd spent my life trying to combat stereotypes and misinformation, it'd make me wary, too. "Thank you." I ended the call and stared at Charlotte. "I'm not making many friends by investigating this."

"That's not your job. Your job is to bring Lacey home."

"You're right, but I hate that this is making me identify with Stone and Wallis just a tiny bit. They were assholes, but at least now I know why they were sniffing around Jax and Kai."

"Those donut-heads wouldn't know justice if it slapped them upside the head. Forget them. They're idiots who more than likely deserve to be behind bars themselves."

I chuckled because that was likely true.

"Knock, knock!" Trish said as she walked in the front door.

"We're in the kitchen," I called and stood to get her a cup of coffee.

When she appeared in the doorway, there was a smile on her face and her eyes were lit with happiness.

"You're in a good mood. Anything we should know about?" I asked her as I handed her the cup of coffee. I gestured for her to take a seat.

Once we were all settled at the table, she took a sip of the coffee, sighed in satisfaction, and said, "Thanks for this."

"Sure. Now, tell us what's up," I said.

"It's Ty. We just had our first weekly meeting yesterday, and I'm just elated. It went so well. We talked and cried and hugged and even have dinner plans with Kennedy and Carson next week." Her eyes misted with tears. "I can't thank you enough, Marion. I just know you're the one who put him up to this, and I want you to know how much I appreciate it."

I blinked at her. "I didn't put him up to anything, Trish."

"Oh, come on. You expect me to believe that he's suddenly done this turn around without a push from you?" She let out a small bark of laughter. "Please. I know my son. When he digs in, he really digs in. It's okay. I know you're behind this."

Irritation curled in my gut, and I wanted to lash out at Trish. She was infantilizing her son, who was a grown man, and it annoyed me to no end. I cleared my throat. "I really didn't. All I know is that he's been seeing a therapist who's been helping him work through his abandonment issues. But that's all work that Ty has done that has nothing to do with me. I wish you'd see that Ty is his own man and capable of making his own decisions."

"Oh, I know he's a man now," she said, waving an unconcerned hand. "But it's obvious the effect you've had on him, and I just wanted to thank you."

It was hard to argue that I hadn't had an effect on him when I'd been his parental figure for the past five years, but that still didn't mean I deserved any credit for the progress they were making in their relationship. In fact, it sounded like they were doing better than Trish and I were. I decided to ignore her comment and got right to the point as to why I'd asked to see her.

"Listen, I asked you over because Charlotte and I are working on a case, and there is reason to believe that a wolf is involved. Obviously I don't think Jax is involved, nor do I think Kai or the pack had anything to do with it. I'm wondering if you know of any other wolves in the area that we should be taking a look at."

"For what case?" she asked, looking suspicious.

"Lacey Riley's disappearance." There was no point in not telling her.

She frowned and shook her head. "I'm not comfortable with this."

"Why not?" Charlotte asked. "We're just trying to track down possible leads in hopes that we can find her."

"Because wolves are not treated fairly by the law. You both have to know that. Sending law enforcement to them is dangerous."

"You think I'm dangerous?" I asked her, trying to ignore the ache in my chest. Why did all the people I loved suddenly think I was a monster? "Why would you think that? You were my best friend, and my boyfriend is also a wolf. Honestly, Trish, it hurts me that you'd say that."

"I'm not trying to hurt you," Trish said as she stood. "But I'm not comfortable with this. I think I better go."

"And all I'm trying to do is find a woman whose life is on the line!" I called after her.

But she didn't turn around. As the door slammed shut, I wanted to scream.

"She's hiding something," Celia said from behind me.

I spun and found the blond ghost standing in my kitchen. "Why do you think that?"

"I just do." Celia stared longingly at the coffee pot. "I miss my java."

"I would too if I were dead," Charlotte said, commiserating with her.

Celia let out a long sigh. "I miss a lot of things. Oh well. At least I can still spy on people." She flashed a mischievous grin. "I'm going to follow Trish and find out what she's not saying."

Jax's objections to her spying on Kai came flooding back, and I almost asked Celia to leave it alone. But a woman's life was on the line, and it was clear that Trish wasn't going to help us. "Okay," I said with a nod. "Report back as soon as you learn anything."

"Aye, aye, Captain." Celia gave me a sloppy salute and then disappeared again.

"Does that ever get disorienting?" Charlotte asked me.

"It used to, but I'm immune now," I said with a half-hearted chuckle. "At least she never pops into my bedroom."

"Not yet, anyway," Charlotte said with a laugh.

I groaned, praying the ghost didn't become a pervy peeper.

CHAPTER 20

Charlotte was doing the breakfast dishes while I wiped down the table when both of our phones started going off.

Sebastian's name flashed on my screen, and I quickly answered it as I heard Charlotte say, "Hey, Denver. What's up?"

I walked into the other room and said, "Tell me you have information for me."

"I have information. I'm sending it right now so you'll have all the details," he said.

"Perfect. What are the highlights?" I sat on my couch and opened my notebook.

"The reason we had trouble finding information on John Vincent is because that's not his birth name."

"It's not?"

"No. It's Francis Jonathon Krass and—"

"Krass!" I cried out. "Tell me he's related to someone named Sharon Krass."

"Sharon is his sister. How did you know that?" Sebastian asked.

I quickly filled him in on the events of the coven meeting from the night before. "Gigi didn't tell you?"

"She said some strange man appeared, but she didn't tell me you knew his name." Sebastian *tsked*. "You need to tell Brix there is something rotten over there at the PPPD."

"Why?"

"Because Sharon Krass is the longtime partner of one Officer J. Stone."

I froze in place. The implications of the revelation were huge. "You're saying that John and Stone's significant other are brother and sister."

"Yes, that's what I'm saying."

No wonder Stone seemed to be covering for him. Or at least not looking too hard. He was trying to keep his partner happy. "Does the document include Sharon's address?"

"You're not going to go over there, are you?" Sebastian asked, concern in his tone.

"Charlotte and I are officially on this case for the MTF. I think we have to," I said.

"You do realize you'll be going up against the entire police department if you target her, right?"

"Are you trying to tell me to stay out of it, Sebastian?" I knew he was worried about me, but this was my job. I didn't have a choice.

"No. Not at all. I just want to make sure you're protected. Have some back up or something."

It was the middle of the day on a Wednesday. None of the coven members were going to be able to drop their work just to go talk to this woman. Besides, I didn't even know if she was involved outside of just trying to protect her brother. "We'll be careful," I promised him. "And if we find anything out that means we have to engage her or Stone, we'll call the MTF for backup."

"Promise?"

"I promise." Damn. My reputation was preceding me.

After we ended the call, I walked back into the kitchen to find my sister on her computer, peering intently at the screen. "What are you looking at, Charlotte?"

My sister jerked her head up, her eyes wide and her lips pressed into a grim line when she turned her laptop around to show me her screen.

The headline read: *Missing Premonition Pointe Woman the Second to Disappear in Less than a Week.*

The picture below it was none other than Lacey's neighbor, Kylie Brickenson.

I let out a sharp gasp. "No! When? How?"

"Last night. Apparently she went for a run just before dark and never returned. Her sister reported her missing around midnight after she never came to pick up her daughter."

"No, no, no, no, no." I shook my head back and forth as if that would change anything. Finally I looked up at my sister and, in a barely audible voice, asked, "Is this our fault?"

"Our *fault?*" Her expression turned stormy. "Definitely not our fault. Whoever took her is entirely to blame."

"You know what I mean. Was she targeted because we went over there yesterday and she talked to us?"

Charlotte's outrage disappeared as she slumped against the couch. "Maybe? Probably." She squeezed her eyes closed, looking as pained as I felt. "But it's still not our fault. You know that, right?"

"Yeah. I do." I stood. "Come on. We have work to do."

She stared up at me. "Where are we going?"

"To track down Sharon Krass. If John took Lacey, then it's highly probable that he came back for Kylie. She's the only one who knew he'd been at Lacey's apartment that morning."

"Who's Sharon?" she asked in confusion, and I realized I hadn't yet filled her in on what happened at the coven meeting or my call with Sebastian.

After getting her up to speed, I went back into the kitchen, opened my laptop, and then scanned the information that Sebastian had sent. After jotting down Sharon's home address and her place of business, I grabbed my phone and said, "Ready?"

"No." Charlotte disappeared into her bedroom. Two minutes later, she was back wearing black leggings and a black sweatshirt.

I glanced down at my jeans and my red T-shirt and went to change. Once I was in my own sneak outfit, I joined Charlotte near the front door. She had my dagger in one hand and a bag of snacks in the other.

"Remind me to give you a raise later," I said, grinning at her.

"Don't worry, I will." She smirked and then led the way out to my SUV.

After I vetoed Charlotte's desire to drive, I climbed into the driver's seat and glanced at the clock. It was just after eleven on a Wednesday. "Do you think she's working or at home?"

"Try work first," Charlotte said as she scrolled through her phone. "It says here that her office is open most days from ten to two."

"Ten to two?" I cried. "Seriously? The woman only works four hours a day?"

"Only sometimes, apparently. It also says to call ahead just to make sure she's in. Must be nice to be an independent accountant."

My thoughts whirled with what an asset Sharon must be if Stone and his partner were actual dirty cops. While we had less than zero amount of evidence that they were doing anything illegal, I had witnessed what appeared to be a drug deal behind the police station the day before. There was no telling what those two were up to.

Charlotte pointed me in the direction of Sharon's office, and within ten minutes we were parked across the street from the unassuming office that happened to be directly across the square from our own offices at the dating agency.

My sister peered out the window. "Should we go in?"

"We aren't going to be able to ask her about her brother from out here." I pushed my door open and was just climbing out of the SUV when a woman stepped out of the office and locked the door behind her. I ducked back into the vehicle and looked over at Charlotte. "That has to be Sharon, right?"

"Looks like her to me." Charlotte held up her phone and pointed it in my direction. The picture on the screen looked like a more put-together version of the woman who'd just left the office.

"Yeah, it's her. Isn't it amazing the things photo filters can do these days?" I mused as I put the SUV in gear.

Sharon had climbed into a sleek Mercedes and was already speeding down Main Street.

"Floor it," Charlotte said.

I refrained from rolling my eyes and did a U-turn right there in the middle of the street so that we could follow the Mercedes through downtown.

"She's got a lead foot," Charlotte mused.

I side-eyed my sister. "She's not the only one."

"I was chasing down a lead. What else was I supposed to do?"

The Mercedes turned right, and I quickly changed lanes so that I could follow.

"Is she headed to the police station?" Charlotte asked, looking worried.

"Doesn't look like it. If she was, she'd have turned already." I kept my eyes on the Mercedes as I tried to pinpoint where she might be going. The road we were on led out of town and into the foothills. There wasn't much out that way except for residential homes and trailheads. There was a town about thirty miles away, but it was small, and the only businesses were a gas station, a convenience store with a sandwich shop, and a dingey bar.

"Maybe the casino?" Charlotte asked.

Right. I'd forgotten all about the casino as I wasn't much of a gambler. "Maybe." Sure enough, fifteen minutes later, Sharon turned into the parking lot of the Cascade Casino. I followed her, but instead of following her to the valet, I held back, opting to park in the lot so that we could keep our distance.

"Look at her, hurrying inside," Charlotte said.

"I guess she needs her fix. Let's go before she gets lost in a sea of slot machines."

We hurried across the lot and into the casino. We were immediately assaulted by the bells and chimes of the slots going off as person after person hit the buttons, eagerly waiting for a payout.

"She's over there!" Charlotte called over the noise.

I followed her gaze and spotted the woman standing next to a man who was feeding a bill into his machine. She looked annoyed as she held out her hand and glared down at him. Finally, the man reached into his wallet and handed her a wad of cash. She counted it quickly, stuffed it into her blouse, and then strode away, heading for the exit.

"That looked like a shakedown," Charlotte said.

"Maybe. Or I suppose it's possible he just owed her some money." I didn't really care about the money. I just wanted to find out where I might look for John and whether Sharon knew anything about his whereabouts. I took off, trying to put myself in Sharon's path, but a large group of gamblers filed out of the buffet, obscuring my view.

"Excuse me. Excuse me," I said over and over again as I tried to fight my way through the crowd. But then a woman slipped right in front of me and grabbed my arm, taking us both down. My elbow hit first and then my backside, sending a shooting pain from my tailbone. "Son of a bitch!" I cried out and rolled to my side, holding my elbow to my frame.

"Marion!" My sister cut through the maze of people and crouched down. "Are you okay? Anything broken? Do we need to take you to the emergency room?"

I sat up, pain throbbing up my arm as I slowly bent the

limb. While my elbow ached, there was no sharp pain or any reason to think anything was broken. "My arm is okay, I think. Let's see if I can stand."

She helped me up, and after a few steps, it was clear I was going to live.

"Where's Sharon?" I asked as I glanced around.

"I don't see her," Charlotte said as she guided me toward the door.

"Dammit. We missed a perfectly good opportunity to talk to her." I ground my teeth together, hoping we could still find her. "Let's go. She's probably either going back to the office or going home."

Charlotte frowned as she looked me up and down. "Are you sure you don't need to go see someone?"

"I'm fine," I insisted, and then I noticed that my black leggings had a run and there was something sticky on my sweatshirt. "Ugh. I look like I've been dumpster diving or something."

"You kinda smell like it too," Charlotte teased.

I elbowed her and then winced when pain shot up my arm again.

"Serves you right," she said.

We hurried as fast as we could out of the casino. And just as we stepped out, we spotted the valet getting out of her Mercedes. She jumped in and sped off.

"Let's go!" I cried as I broke into a run, holding my sore elbow to my body.

When we got to the car, Charlotte shoved me out of the way and took the driver's side. "You have a broken wing. I'm driving."

My arm was throbbing, so I didn't protest. As soon as I was in the SUV, she took off like a bat out of hell. I gripped the oh "shit handle" again and prayed to the goddess that we'd get back to town safely.

Luckily, the road only had a few hairy turns, and by the time I saw the familiar sights of Premonition Pointe, I was confident we weren't going to be found in a ditch on the two-lane highway.

"Looks like she's headed back to work," Charlotte said when the Mercedes took the turn for downtown instead of the one that would head north toward the house that had been in Sebastian's file.

"I think she's getting lunch first." I pointed to the fast food burger joint as Sharon pulled into the drive-through.

"I could eat," Charlotte said and made the turn, following her.

"Park in the lot and I'll go in and grab something. We can't be stuck in the drive-through when she leaves."

"Fine." Charlotte pulled into a parking space and hit the brakes, making the seatbelt nearly choke me.

"A little finesse next time please. Text me if she's taking off." I jumped out of the car and ran into the burger place. Luckily there was no line. I ordered two burgers, two fries, and two drinks, hoping that my uncomplicated order would mean I wasn't waiting forever.

Sure enough, right after I paid, the server handed me my food and two cups. I was just finishing filling the second soda when the text came through.

She's at the pickup window.

I hurried out and got back in the SUV. "Made it," I said.

"You didn't get me a milkshake?" Charlotte stared at me with puppy dog eyes.

"I went for simple. Be happy you got anything at all."

"Ketchup?"

"It's in the bag," I said, shoving it at her.

Charlotte was busy dabbing ketchup on her fries when Sharon's Mercedes pulled away from the window.

"Time to go," I said, snatching the packet out of her hand and sending a blob of ketchup onto her sleeve.

"It's better than whatever I'm sporting," I said before she could complain, gesturing to the sticky sweatshirt I was still wearing. "Now get moving before we lose her again."

Sharon sped down Main Street, passed her office, and turned into an older neighborhood with cottages that sat on a hill and had distant views of the ocean. We followed her through the neighborhood and then back down to Main Street.

"What is she—" I started.

Whoop. Whoop. The sound of sirens blared through the air, and suddenly there were flashing lights behind us.

"Shit." Charlotte pulled the SUV to the side of the road and glanced around. "Hand me my wallet."

I did as she asked and waited for the cop to come give her the ticket she so rightfully deserved. But instead of going to the driver's side, the cop knocked on my window. I quickly lowered it and looked right into the face of Officer Stone.

"Ms. Matched," he said, his expression full of rage. "Why are you stalking Ms. Krass?"

Interesting that he called her Ms. Krass. Was he

unwilling to admit that they'd been partners for years. "Stalking?" I scoffed. "That's not what I was doing at all."

"Did you or did you not follow her all the way to Cascade Casino and then back into town?"

"Well, yes, but we weren't stalking her. I just wanted to ask her a few questions about her brother John," I said just to see what his reaction would be.

"How did you—" He cleared his throat as his face turned bright red. "I suggest you leave Ms. Krass and her brother alone, Ms. Matched. You wouldn't want anything to happen to that shifter of yours, I'm sure."

"Was that another threat?" I shot back.

"It sounds like it, doesn't it?" His lips curved into a sinister smile. "It wouldn't take much to pin those abductions on him."

"You've got nothing on Jax." My entire body was vibrating because of his audacity.

"No, not yet, but it sure would be a shame if some evidence just appeared, wouldn't it?"

"Trust me when I say this, Officer Stone; if anything like that happens, I will take the entire department down. Understand?"

"You could try, I suppose." He smirked. "But doubtful. In any case, all you need to do is stay away from Ms. Krass and her brother, and you won't have anything to worry about." Then he strolled back to his patrol car and left us on the side of the road.

"Well, that was creepy," Charlotte said.

"Very." I stared at the police car until it disappeared around a corner. There was no doubt in my mind that Stone wasn't just protecting Sharon. He'd made a point of telling me to stay away from John, too.

Charlotte started the SUV. "That was a bust. Where to now?"

"Home. I think we need to regroup."

CHAPTER 21

"Coffee?" I asked Charlotte as she fed Minx a treat.

"Got Irish cream to go in it?" she asked without even looking up.

"I wish." I walked over to the refrigerator to double check that I didn't have a bottle hiding in there and shut it in disappointment.

"Fine. I'll have coffee with regular creamer instead," she said with a sigh as she slumped into a chair at the table. "I can't believe Stone threatened Jax like that. The weasel. If I get my hands on him, I'll—"

"I'm back!" Celia said, popping into the kitchen for the second time that day. "Did you miss me?"

"Yes," Both Charlotte and I said at the same time.

"You did?" She beamed at us. "That's sweet. I think I'm growing on you two."

"That must be it." Honestly, after the morning we'd had, I was just happy for the distraction.

"What do you have for us, Celia?" Charlotte asked as she pulled a box of cookies out of the pantry.

I held my hand out, indicating I wanted the cookies.

"Keep your grubby hands to yourself," Charlotte said. "I'll get you a couple in a minute."

"I want a cookie," Celia said, staring longingly at the bag.

"Of course you do, honey." Charlotte gave her a sympathetic smile. "We all want them."

Charlotte took a stack of four for herself and then handed me two. I grimaced at her but kept my thoughts to myself. Four cookies were more than my ass needed anyway.

"Well?" Charlotte said through her cookie crumbs.

"I found out where Trish is staying." Celia beamed with pride.

"Okay, where, and why is that important?" I asked and then took a sip of my coffee to wash down the cookie.

Looking rather pleased with herself, Celia said, "She's staying at a camp north of here about ten miles. And guess who's with her?"

"Uh... I dunno, a couple of strippers from Abs, Buns, and Guns?" I asked cheekily.

Celia actually snorted out a laugh. "That would be a lot more entertaining, but no. She's sharing her camp with two other shifters."

I sat up so abruptly that my coffee sloshed onto my sticky sweatshirt.

"Goddess above, Marion," Celia said, eyeing me. "What in the world are you wearing? Are you trying out for a part in *Little Orphan Annie* or something?"

Charlotte snickered. "She had a little accident earlier

when she was run over by a mob of buffet enthusiasts. It wasn't pretty."

"What'd you do? Get between them and the cheesecake?" Celia asked me.

"Ha-ha. Very funny. I slipped and fell and haven't had a chance to change. So sue me. Now what's this about Trish living with two other wolves?"

"It's two women who appear to be together and then Trish, who mostly keeps trying to ask about their background and how they ended up in Premonition Pointe. But they're being evasive. Seems suspicious to me."

Charlotte and I glanced at each other and stood at the same time.

"Looks like we need to pay someone a visit," I told Celia. "Do you have an address for me?"

"I have a description of the location. Addresses aren't really assigned to makeshift camps," she said.

"Right." I headed for the door, more than ready to have something other than my run-in with Stone to focus on.

"Hold on," Charlotte said, grabbing my wrist. "You can't go like that."

"Like what?"

"Like a homeless person," she said, crossing her arms over her chest. "Go change or I'm leaving you behind."

"That's rich since we both know you won't drive your car."

"I drive my car," she insisted.

"Not out of town and definitely not up in the woods. You'd be complaining about the gas cost the entire way," I called as I headed to my bedroom, more than ready to lose the sticky sweatshirt. When I was back and dressed in another pair of black leggings and a clean steel blue sweatshirt, I turned to Celia. "Can you come along and guide us?"

The ghost bobbed up and down with excitement. "I get to go on a stakeout?!"

"It's not a stakeout," Charlotte said, shaking her head. "It's an interrogation."

The ghost brought her hands together in a silent clap. "Even better. I can be the bad cop."

Charlotte laughed. "You? No way. They'd laugh in your pretty little face. Marion's the bad cop. She has that mom face down pat."

"Mom face?" I raised an eyebrow in her direction and then just shook my head. "There's no need for good cops or bad cops. This is an interview, not an interrogation. We're not accusing anyone of anything, got it?"

"She's really a stick-in-the-mud, isn't she?" Celia asked Charlotte while we were on our way out.

"You can say that again." They both broke out in giggles, and I ignored them as I went for the driver's side door.

"I'm driving," Charlotte said, trying to push me out of the way.

"No. I've got it. My arm is sore, but it's not debilitating anymore. I'll drive my own car. But if you want to drive, we can go in yours—"

"Never mind. Yours is more comfortable." Charlotte held the back door open for Celia, but the ghost completely ignored her. And instead of floating into the SUV, she momentarily popped out of existence and reappeared in the back seat, right in the middle so she could see both of us.

"Why do I always forget she can do that?" Charlotte asked no one in particular as we both got into the car.

"Beats me. It's not like she doesn't do it at least once a day lately," I said and glanced back at the ghost. "Where to, Ms. Maps?"

"North on 101," she said.

Twenty-five minutes later, we were moving slowly down an unmaintained dirt road that I strongly suspected was a fire road. "Are you sure we're going the right way?" I asked Celia.

"I'm positive. I'm dead, not stupid."

Charlotte chuckled softly. "I hope I have her attitude once I kick the bucket."

"Stick with me, girlfriend," Celia said as she leaned in closer. "Imagine the people we could haunt."

They both looked at me.

"What would make that any different than what I deal with on a daily basis?" I asked and gritted my teeth when we rolled over a deep pothole.

"There it is!" Celia said, pointing through the trees to the left.

I stepped on the brakes and peered through the redwoods. I couldn't see anything except shadows and decided that if they were living there, it was a damned good hiding spot. It reminded me of a secret fairy garden. "Let's go."

Charlotte and I climbed out of the SUV while Celia did her vanishing trick only to turn up right in front of me when she reappeared.

"Follow me," Celia said and floated through the trees.

Just as she entered the hidden area, an arrow came flying out of nowhere and struck the tree right next to me.

Charlotte and I froze.

"That was just rude," Celia called out. "I'm a ghost. You can't kill me that way."

"Ghost?" a female voice called from the secret garden.

"Yeah. I died, so now I'm a ghost. What's so hard to comprehend?" Celia sounded impatient, and if I didn't interrupt the conversation, who knew what could happen?

"I'm looking for Trish Kirkwood," I called out.

"Marion?" My friend popped out of the secret garden with her face scrunched up in confusion. "How did you find us here?"

I waved at Celia. "She followed you."

Trish glared at the ghost. "If I had any sage on me, you'd be history."

"Like I want to stay in your damp camp anyway." Celia waggled her fingers at me and Charlotte and then disappeared again.

"I really don't like her," Trish said as she stomped back through the trees.

"Is it safe to follow her?" Charlotte asked me.

"I have no idea." I took one hesitant step forward. When no arrows flew out of the clearing, I took another one.

"Just get in here," Trish called.

"No one's going to shoot us, are they?" Charlotte asked.

Trish made an irritated noise and then answered, "Not yet. But no promises."

"That's reassuring," Charlotte muttered.

I led the way into the damp clearing and glanced around. Sure enough, there were two tents. One was pretty large, plenty big enough for two people, and the other looked barely large enough for one person to stretch out. "This is where you're staying?"

"We were, but now that Celia knows where we are, we might have to move," Trish said, her annoyance unmistakable.

"Celia isn't going to out you to anyone. She works for me," I said.

"Is that right?" Trish placed her hands on her hips and glared at me. "So you ordered her to surveil me when I wouldn't tell you where I was staying?"

"No. Not exactly," I hedged. Trish continued to glare at me until I caved and finally came clean. "Celia took it upon herself, and I just didn't stop her."

"That's... awful, Marion." Trish shook her head and went to sit on a log near her tent.

"Is it more awful than letting me speak to your two companions when I'm trying to find a missing woman?" I asked.

"*Two* missing women," Charlotte corrected.

"Right. Two," I repeated.

"What?" Trish stood and walked over to us. "What do you mean, two women? Who else went missing?"

"Lacey's neighbor disappeared right after we talked to her and learned that Lacey's ex had been at her apartment the morning she disappeared," I explained.

Trish pressed her hand to her throat and shook her head slightly. "That's terrible. What can I do to help?"

Wasn't it obvious? I was there to talk to her two wolf friends. Praying for patience, I said, "We think a wolf may have been involved when Lacey went missing. All we want to know is if any of you know of any problematic wolves that might be nearby. One who might not care what happens to a stranger."

There was a rustle of foliage, and then a brown-skinned woman appeared. She was wearing tight jeans, a crop top, and hiking boots. Her long black hair was plaited in a braid, and she had the longest eyelashes I'd ever seen. Another woman appeared behind her. She was a few inches taller than the first and had thick, long blond hair that reached past her butt. She was dressed in a similar outfit as her friend. Jeans and a crop top.

The one with black hair stepped forward. "Jessa is in town."

Trish spun to stare at her, slack-jawed. "Kai's Jessa?"

She nodded as she worried the end of her braid. "I saw her out on a run the other day out in the woods."

"Did she see you?" Trish demanded.

"I don't think so," the woman said. "But I can't be sure."

Trish glanced back at me. "That's your suspect. Jessa Benson. She's the worst kind of wolf."

Both of the other shifters nodded.

I wasn't sure what that meant exactly, but we were going to get to the root of it before anyone left. I walked up and held my hand out to the dark-haired shifter. "Hi, I'm Marion. I own the Miss Matched Dating Agency, and in my spare time, I work for the Magical Task Force, tracking down bad guys."

"Hi," she said tentatively. "I'm Dannika, and this"—she waved at the shifter with blond hair–"is Zoe, my girlfriend."

"It's nice to meet you, Dannika," I said shaking her hand. Then I turned to Zoe and said, "It's lovely to meet you, Zoe."

Trish huffed out a breath. "This isn't a tea party. No need to be so formal."

I ignored her and met Dannika's gaze. "You know Jessa?"

"We've… met," she said and looked away.

"Do you think she's capable of abducting two women?"

Dannika let out a huff. "Capable? Yes. Is it probable? Definitely. Jessa is the worst kind of wolf, always caving to her worst instincts."

"Do you think Kai knows she's in town?"

"I have no idea. I didn't see him with her when she was out running," Dannika said with a shrug.

"Kai doesn't know," Trish insisted. "If he did, he'd have already run her out of town. After what she did to him, he'd never even consider letting her back into his good graces."

I could believe that. Kai seemed like a decent man, but he definitely wasn't weak, and I could imagine he was harboring some deep resentment toward her.

"You think Jessa is abducting people?" Zoe asked. Her entire body was trembling, and she looked like a frightened rabbit.

"I think it's possible. I just don't know why," I said. "Do you have any ideas?"

Zoe shook her head and then hurried over to the larger tent. She pulled the flap open and climbed in. A moment later, she had her duffle out and was filling it with clothes.

Dannika frowned at her girlfriend and then at me. "If there's any money in it, Jessa would do it. That's all you need to know." The dark-haired wolf joined Zoe, and together they quickly started dismantling their tent.

"What are you doing?" Trish asked as she rushed over to them. "You're not leaving just because of Jessa, are you?"

"Yes," Zoe said. "I've been in trouble before because of her. I'm not sticking around to see what destruction she causes this time." She looked at me. "Be careful. Jessa is the type to do just about anything to stay free of the law."

"What else has she done?" Charlotte asked, looking horrified.

"You name it. She's done it." Zoe slung her duffle over her shoulder as Dannika hefted a large backpack that contained their tent onto her back. A few moments later, the pair walked off into the woods.

"Wait!" Trish raced after them. "You don't have to leave. Marion is really good at fighting bad guys and making things right."

"I'm sorry, Trish," Dannika called back. "We just can't risk it."

After they were gone, Trish slumped down on her log and buried her face in her hands. "I can't believe this. It can't be true."

"What? That they left or that Jessa is here?" I asked gently.

"Both." She jerked her head up. "Jessa is evil incarnate. Kai is going to lose his mind. And they're right. If there are bad things happening in Premonition Pointe, it's likely due to her."

"But why would she come here?" I asked.

"To torture Kai and make his life miserable?" She threw her hands up. "I don't know." Then she looked around and sighed. "I guess I better pack up. I can't stay here now."

"Why?" Charlotte asked.

"It's not safe for just one person." She got busy packing and then out of nowhere started to explain. "You see, ever since I shifted into a wolf, I don't like enclosed spaces. It makes me feel... trapped, I guess. I just feel better if I'm living and sleeping outdoors. But I can't afford a regular campground, so I've been here. Or sometimes down at the beach. That was fine when Zoe and Dannika were here. There's strength in numbers. But a single female shifter by herself? That's a recipe for trouble."

"Any idea where you'll go?" I asked, wishing I could invite her back to the house. But I'd have to ask Ty first, and besides, it wasn't exactly outdoor living.

"To the Diablo pack, I guess. I know Kai will let me set up a temporary camp somewhere on his land." She glanced around the clearing one last time before she turned to me. "Care to give me a ride? I've been borrowing Dannika's car for a while since mine needs a new alternator and I can't afford to get it fixed right now."

"Sure." I put my arm around her and gave her a sideways hug. "I'm sorry about Celia."

She waved a hand. "Forget it. I know you're just doing what you have to do. So am I."

"Life sure got complicated in our old age, didn't it?" I said in a light tone.

"You can say that again." She smiled and leaned into me.

"That's it. I'm never getting old. Forget it," Charlotte announced. "I'm staying in my twenties for forever."

"How? Unlimited supply of Botox?" I asked.

Trish glanced at her. "Maybe she plans to be a ghost like Celia."

"She better not!" I stared at my sister. "Right?"

Charlotte laughed. "I'm not looking to off myself for eternal youth. I was thinking more like fillers and plastic surgery. Maybe a beauty potion here and there. Stop freaking."

"I'm not freaking," I lied. The truth was that anything was possible. I'd seen so much crazy crap the past year, I wasn't ruling anything out. "But I am holding you to that. Filler and Botox. That's it."

"And maybe a nip and tuck," she added with a wink.

"I'm not sure how that's gonna keep you from experiencing some shit, but at least you'll be pretty while doing it," Trish said and then chuckled.

"Damn straight," Charlotte agreed. And once again, my pushy sister tried to climb into the driver's seat.

I pointed to the back. "For that you get to ride back there. Get in."

"You're no fun." But she did as I asked and then peered through the seats just like Celia had earlier. "Where to now?"

"Kai's," I said. "We need to figure out how to find Jessa."

CHAPTER 22

"*W*here is everyone?" Trish asked as we came to a stop in front of the old barn at Gray Wolf Winery.

I glanced around, spotting Jax's work truck and a silver Toyota 4Runner. There were no other vehicles, and none of the pack were wandering around. All three of us got out of the SUV and made our way into the barn. The lights were on, and there was coffee in the coffee maker, though it was cold and looked like it hadn't been touched since that morning.

"Maybe they made a supply run," Charlotte said.

"All of them?" I asked. "And in whose truck?"

"What? Do you think I'm a Magic 8 Ball and have all the answers?" Charlotte shot back. "I'm just brainstorming here."

"Sorry," I muttered. "I just don't like the looks of this. It feels… off."

"Smells off, too," Trish said, sniffing the air like a scent hound. "It smells like... like sandalwood mixed with patchouli."

Charlotte sniffed and immediately made a gagging noise. "Patchouli should be illegal. That stuff makes my eyes water like I'm locked in a room with twenty cats."

"That is bad," I said, knowing how allergic she was to the sweet animals.

"Kai doesn't use sandalwood or Patchouli," Trish said. "I'd remember those scents."

"So someone else was here," I mused.

"Someone with bad taste in cologne," Charlotte quipped.

Trish started searching each of the rooms in the old barn, calling out for Kai and Jax. Charlotte and I joined her. There was nothing. No movement. No shifters. No sound.

Until we got to the very last old stall. Trish opened the door, and all three of us let out a collective gasp.

Trish was the first to recover, and she fell to her knees to shake one of the five shifters who were lying unconscious in a heap on the floor. All of them wore various forms of clothing that looked as if it had ripped, maybe while trying to shift. But they were all in human form now and looked less than helpless.

"Are they breathing?" Charlotte asked, her voice barely a whisper.

"They are," Trish said, sounding relieved. "They've been hit with some sort of magical sleeping potion."

"Can we wake them up?" I asked, reaching for the closest one. Ryder was his name. I recognized him from when I'd toured the property.

"You can try," Trish said. "If it's a spell you might be able to break it, but if it's a potion, probably not."

As a witch, I'd already known that, but I appreciated her reminding me. I held Ryder's hand in mine and tried to see if I could pull the curse from him. But nothing I did worked. All I got was a queasy feeling from the rancid energy that was radiating off him. "It's not working. Whatever this is, we either need to call the coven in or wait it out."

"Probably wait it out," Trish said. "If whoever did this wanted them dead, they'd already be gone. Leave them. They'll come out of it sooner rather than later. Hopefully they won't suffer any side effects after they wake up. Right now, we need to look for clues for how to find Kai and Jax."

I pulled my phone out and immediately called Jax, but his phone went straight to voice mail. The same thing happened when I tried Kai. "Dammit!" I cried.

"You didn't think it'd be that easy, did you?" Trish asked as she stared at me, looking perplexed.

"No, but I had to try." I glanced back down the hall and then said, "Come on. I have an idea."

"What idea?" Charlotte asked.

"I think I know how to find out what happened to them." I rushed to Kai's office and then sat down at his computer. Thankfully there was no screen lock, however, when I clicked the link for the security cameras, it was password protected. "Crap. What would Kai use as a password?"

Trish and Charlotte stared at me blankly.

"Hello, I need to see his security footage, but I can't do that unless we hack his computer. Now, start brainstorming."

"Ohhhh," Charlotte said. "I get it now." She rattled off the most obvious things a person could muster, including Kai#1 and AlphasRule.

"Maybe something a little less obvious?" I said.

"Use PoundPuppy2012," Trish said.

I glanced back at her. "Are you serious?"

"Yep." She tapped a picture frame on the shelf behind her. "It's Kai with his little brother before he was cut off by his family because of his status. The signature off to the side is *PoundPuppy2012*."

"His parents cut him off because he was cursed with the wolf bite?" I asked, horrified. I couldn't imagine cutting off my loved ones for any reason, especially when they'd had no choice about becoming a wolf. It was barbaric and just plain heartbreaking.

"Yeah. Sucks, right?" Trish said.

I tried the PoundPuppy password and just like that, the screen came up. I quickly searched the cameras for any activity and finally hit paydirt with the one that was installed outside Kai's office in the barn.

"What is that?" Charlotte asked as she peered over my shoulder. "Fog?"

"No," I said. "It's smoke. From a smoke bomb. See it there?" I pointed at the black contraption that was barely visible from the corner as the smoke got thicker and thicker. There was coughing, followed by Kai swearing. And then there was a cackle that sounded like something straight out of a horror film. The lights flickered, and then Jax walked in.

My heart started to pound against my chest, and I desperately wished I could warn him. But just as the thought crossed my mind, Jax crumpled to the floor, looking exactly like the men at the other end of the barn.

I was nearly in full panic mode, wondering if I'd just overlooked Jax among the other unconscious shifters.

No. That didn't happen. That could never happen. I just felt a pull when he was around. I assumed it would be the same even if he was still deep under.

Movement on the screen caught my eye. Someone reached over and tugged at Jax's feet, moving him off camera. I pressed my fingertips to the screen as if that could stop them and had to fight back tears of anger. How dare they do that to Jax? Hauling him around like a sack of potatoes. It was just wrong. Inhuman.

"What's that?" Trish asked, pointing to a shadowy figure at the top of the screen. They were petite and wearing jeans and a T-shirt. For the entire video, the person managed to stay just out of range of the camera until right at the end.

Trish paused it, giving us a decent view of the person's face despite it being a little blurry.

"That's Fiona!" I cried, jabbing my finger on the screen.

"Fiona, the neighbor, Fiona?" Charlotte clarified.

"Yes, Fiona the neighbor. I don't know why she did this. Why did she set off a smoke bomb? What's the end game?" I spewed as thoughts whirled in my head.

"There's only one way to find out," Trish said as she headed for the door. "Let's ask her."

I stared at my friend, unable to process what was happening. Jax was gone. Kai was gone. And somehow, the grouchy neighbor seemed to be the prime suspect.

"You coming?" Trish asked, one eyebrow raised.

"Yeah. I'm coming."

"Me, too," Charlotte chimed in, and together we trudged across the property and walked right up on Fiona's porch and rang the doorbell.

We were greeted by a hunting rifle and four words. "Get off my property."

CHAPTER 23

J felt Charlotte shift to move behind me, and just when I thought she was using me as a shield, she took my hand and pressed the cool handle of my dagger into it. Bless her for remembering to bring the one thing that could possibly get us out of this mess.

"Where are Kai and Jax?" I demanded.

Fiona pointed the weapon at me. "You're not welcome here. Go now, or I'm calling the PPPD."

I contemplated letting her do just that, but considering the warning Stone had given me and Charlotte only a few hours earlier, I didn't think that would go well for us.

"We know you set the smoke bombs next door," Trish snarled.

"Stop talking nonsense," Fiona said, sounding irritated. "I don't know what you're trying to pin on me, but I'm not standing for it. Understand?"

"We have video," Trish pressed.

"Ha! Like video means anything anymore. *If* you have

something like that, and it's a big *if*, then I'm guessing it's AI. You know they can do just about anything with video these days."

"Fiona—" I started, but then I shut my mouth when she released the safety on her gun. "Never mind." I took a step back. "Let's just go. Clearly we aren't going to get anywhere here."

Trish whirled on me. "But, Marion, we can't just let her get away—"

I held my free hand up, stopping her. "We don't want any trouble. Let's go."

"At least one of you has a brain," Fiona spat before she stepped back into her house and slammed the door.

"I can't believe we're just leaving," Trish growled at me as I led the way back to the winery.

"Shhh," I hushed. "It was a mistake to come here like this. We need to regroup." I didn't know what I'd been thinking, heading over to Fiona's half-cocked without a plan. This was a woman who'd orchestrated an attack on the pack, knocked out most of the members, and presumably abducted Kai and Jax. What did I think she was going to do, open the doors wide and invite us in? I'd been so angry that I hadn't thought any of it through. Actually, I'd let Trish lead, and that had proven to be a mistake.

"Idiot," I muttered to myself, already pulling out my phone and calling Brix. This was bigger than just me and my two sidekicks. The call went straight to voice mail, making me curse.

"Who are you calling an idiot?" Charlotte asked as she glanced at Trish.

Trish flipped her off.

"Me. That was beyond reckless. What we need is a plan. We need to do recon. And we need backup." I stomped into the old barn and took a seat at Kai's desk.

"Who said you're in charge?" Trish challenged. "This is wolf business."

I glared at her. "The Magical Task Force put me in charge, Trish. Like it or not, Charlotte and I actually do have the authority to call the shots. If you want to help, fine. I welcome that. But if you're going to fight me on this, then I'm going to have to insist that you stand down. Because it doesn't get more serious than this. Jax is missing. So is Kai. And we have a room full of wolves that have been magically subdued. We have no idea when they are going to come out of it either. Plus, Jessa is out there, and if she's involved in this, it sounds like we have a royal mess on our hands."

Trish stared at me for a long moment and then sank slowly into one of the chairs, her face white. "We just made a huge mistake, didn't we?"

"Maybe not," Charlotte said as she glanced at the door to the office. "Isn't it interesting that Fiona was caught on camera?"

"What do you mean interesting?" I asked her, wondering where she was going with this.

"Look at her again," Charlotte said.

We gathered around the computer, and I hit Play on the recording.

"See how she looks right into the camera and pauses for just a moment? It's almost as if she *wants* to be seen. I think she's baiting us."

"You mean she wants us to know it was her that did this?" I asked Charlotte.

"I think so. She didn't have to look at the camera. If she'd just kept her head down and walked in, we never would have known who that was. Fiona does not strike me as a woman who makes mistakes like that."

"I don't know. She was pretty unreasonable about the pipe that was cut. She seems irrational to me," I said.

"She's an old busybody who hates wolves," Trish added. "I don't think it's that complicated."

"There's only one way to find out," I said. "We need to do a recon mission and figure out what's going on over there at Fiona's farm."

"Tonight?" Charlotte asked.

"Tonight," I confirmed. Whatever Fiona was up to, I wasn't waiting a second longer to find out what happened to Jax.

"Just us three?" Trish asked, looking both ready to spring into action and slightly worried.

"I'm going to leave a message for Brix and let the coven know what we're up to. But we're not going to plan any sort of attack. I just want to know what we're dealing with. Once we do, we'll call in everyone we can," I said.

Charlotte nodded. "Sounds good."

"I don't like it," Trish said, shaking her head. "Are you telling me that if we find Jax being tortured that you're not going to try to stop it?"

I ground my teeth together. Trish had a point. Would I be able to retreat if I saw something heinous going on? I wasn't sure I could. But how could we plan an attack without knowing what we were walking into? "Honestly, I don't know, Trish. But we can't just bust in there. We'd likely get ambushed or arrested or both."

"Fine," she said. "But don't say I didn't warn you."

"STICK CLOSE TO ME," I told my two cohorts as we crept along the southeastern edge of the property line. After studying Kai's security footage, we were able to roughly identify where Kai's land stopped and Fiona's started. "We need to figure out if there are alarms and security cameras before we head onto Fiona's property."

"We're not going anywhere until you tell us to," Charlotte said.

I gestured for her to stand next to me and then held out my dagger. She grabbed it with her right hand, and we both held on as I conjured up a spell. "Goddess of light and darkness, show us safe passage. Keep us safe and hidden as we enter the lands of the unknown."

A small clap of thunder rumbled overhead, and suddenly a mass of green glowing fireflies appeared on the property with a few paths of darkness winding through the spectacle.

"Whoa. That was impressive," Trish said, awe in her tone.

"That was pretty cool," Charlotte added. "Where'd you learn that one?"

"At one of the coven meetings. We've been practicing various spells. I ran across this one in an old spell book that Brix gave me and asked them to help me refine it. Looks like it worked. Just stay in darkness out of the range of the fireflies and hopefully we won't trip any alarms. Got it?"

"Got it," they said at the same time.

"Let's each take a path and meet back here in ten

minutes with what we found. Text if you get into any trouble. Just make sure you have your ringers turned off," I ordered.

The three of us checked our phones, and then on my signal, we snuck our way onto Fiona's property.

Careful to stay in my darkness bubble, I crept along, trying to peer out onto Fiona's property. I knew she was supposed to have lavender fields and bee hives, but as far as I could tell, there wasn't anything planted, and I couldn't see any bee houses among the fireflies. The land was cleared, though. The house was off in the distance, illuminated by one window light. And although I couldn't see it, I knew there was a large barn and a garage with at least six bays directly to the south of the house.

A text came in. I glanced at it to see it was from Charlotte. *I don't see anything yet. What about you two?*

Nothing, I typed back. *We're going to need to check the structures. I'm heading that way now.*

I'll check the house, Trish replied.

Be careful. I sent the message and prayed she didn't find herself on the barrel end of Fiona's rifle again.

I was about halfway to the barn when a light caught my attention off to my left. It was brighter than the fireflies. As I moved closer, I could make out lit torches that circled a clearing. And right in the middle was Jax. His wrists were bound over his head and tied to a tree limb, leaving him dangling there while Fiona held a gun to his head.

"No!" I cried out, hearing both Charlotte and Trish scream the same thing.

The fireflies disappeared, and suddenly I saw the scene flicker; Jax turned into Ty and then into me. Confused, I shook my head, trying to clear it. And once again, Jax was staring at me, his eyes vacant as if he didn't even recognize me. Below him had been earth, but now it was a dark pit. Nothing I saw could be trusted. My heart started to pound, and blood rushed to my ears. Then everything became clear. "It's an illusion!" I called out. "They've set a trap. Retreat, retreat!" I ordered.

Charlotte, who was to my left and had been running toward the scene, froze. But Trish had already shifted and was running flat out toward the circle.

I broke into a sprint, not at all confident I could catch a wolf, but thankfully I'd been closer to the circle than she was, so I just managed to get right in front of her before she crossed over into the circle. "It's a trap, Trish. It's not real!" I cried.

The wolf tried to slide to a stop, but her momentum was too much, and she slid right into me, knocking me backward.

I felt like I was falling in slow motion, reaching out for someone to catch my hand, but it was too late. Unable to grab onto anything, I lost my balance and fell backward into the black pit, landing with a loud *thunk*. My head spun, and as I struggled to breathe, my world faded to black.

CHAPTER 24

I woke to the stench of damp earth and ammonia. My eyes were blurry, and I wondered if I had a concussion. Groaning, I tried to push myself up as every muscle in my body protested. Where the hell was I?

It took a moment for my eyes to focus in the dim light, but when they did and I spotted the bars of my cell, I wished I'd stayed unconscious. It wasn't a regular cinderblock cell, the kind one would find at the Premonition Pointe Police department. This was different. The prison had been built below ground, with the cells carved out of the earth. Everywhere I looked was damp dirt. The floor, the walls, the ceiling. Everything except the bars locking me in.

"Marion," a cheerful voice called.

I looked past my cell door and spotted a familiar woman with long blond hair and a flowy white dress. "Lacey!" I jumped up, ignoring the pain pounding in my head that normally would have brought me to my knees. "Are you all right? What happened? How did you end up here?"

"Of course I'm all right." She smiled pleasantly at me. "Why wouldn't I be?"

"Uh, because you went missing days ago and no one knew where you were?"

"I'm not missing. I'm right here." She opened a small slot in the cell door and slid a tray through with what looked to be some sort of broth, a piece of bread, and a bottle of water.

"What about Cody?" I asked, trying to understand why she seemed so at peace.

"Cody?" She stared past me and then frowned in concentration. "You know, that name sounds familiar, but I just can't place it. Is he a friend of yours?"

An ache formed in my gut. Someone had wiped Cody from her memory. If they'd done that, what else had they done to her? "Lacey, where are we?"

"Oh." She brightened. "We're at the Bee Purple Oasis. Isn't it gorgeous?"

I glanced around at the dingey earthen walls, the single bulb lights, and most importantly, the bars that were keeping me locked up, and I couldn't say that I agreed. "The Bee Purple Oasis?"

"Oh, you know. It's a nod to the lavender fields and honeybee farm Fiona's granddaddy used to have before Fiona turned it into this." She waved her hand as if she were showing off a master painting instead of a dungeon. "That's why the walls are covered in lavender."

They most definitely were *not* covered in lavender. Or anything else for that matter. "What has Fiona done to you?"

"Done?" She shook her head. "I don't know what you

mean. Fiona is the kindest, most loving mentor a girl could ask for. You'll see."

I stared at her, realizing there was something unnatural about her smile and that her eyes were a little glazed. Was she on something? "Lacey, how long have you been here?"

"Huh?" She frowned, looking confused. "What do you mean?"

"How many days have you been at the Bee Purple Oasis?" I clarified.

"Oh, that's a silly question, isn't it? I've been here my whole life." She grinned and then glided away as if she didn't have a care in the world.

I sat back in my cell, dumbfounded. Someone powerful had glamoured her. Someone more powerful than I was.

"I TOLD you to stay off my land," Fiona said from behind her desk in a wooden cottage that was hidden in the forest behind her farm. Not long after Lacey had left, some of Fiona's goons had come for me. They'd cuffed and shackled me and then tossed me onto a 4-wheeler and taken me to what I assumed was Fiona's office.

"I wouldn't have come if you hadn't abducted Jax and Kai," I countered.

She grinned like the Cheshire cat. "You don't say."

I glared at her. "Was this all an elaborate trap to get me here, locked up in your shitty dungeon?"

"It's an oasis, Marion." Her snide grin made my skin crawl.

"Yeah, I heard. You didn't answer my question."

She shrugged. "You were being a busybody. It's not my fault you fell into the pit. You got what you deserved."

I stared down at my bound wrists, anger eating at me from the inside out. "Is that what Lacey deserved? To be glamoured and held against her will?"

"Lacey came to me looking for a job. I gave her one. Though we did disagree on her start time. I obviously wanted her to start immediately. She wanted to think it over. Jessa and I made the decision for her shortly after that unfortunate flat tire. As far as I'm concerned, it was a win-win."

"Jessa? Kai's ex works for you?" I asked, surprised since she'd seem to hate Kai and the pack so much, though I supposed I shouldn't be. If Jessa was as corrupt as everyone claimed, she would fit right in with Fiona's ilk.

"Delicious, isn't it? I dare say she is loving torturing him right now. It's nice when my employees get to have a little fun."

"You're despicable," I said, stating the obvious. "Let Lacey go. She has a son to raise."

The older woman leaned back in her chair and eyed me. "You must've noticed that Lacey isn't in a cell. That's hardly holding her against her will. In fact, it looks to me like she could walk off this property any time she wants to. But she won't. She's happy here. I've given her a good life."

"Is that what you think? That she wants to be away from her son?" The hatred I felt for this shell of a human in front of me was unfathomable. As if glamouring people wasn't just a prettier way of locking them up.

"Her life was harder when she was raising her son by herself. I've just taken the pressure off."

"You're not going to get away with this. You know that, right?" I challenged. "I won't let you."

She chuckled. "It's always so entertaining to see how the strong ones react." Confidence radiated off her as she added, "You can try, but you won't succeed. Nothing is going to stop our mining operation here, least of all you."

"Mines? What mines?" What the hell had I stepped into?

"Oh, didn't I tell you? There's a gold mine in these mountains. We mine it to make Gold Rush. Since it's a dangerous job, we're always looking to hire. Luckily for me, desperate men and women keep falling right into my lap. Isn't that fortuitous? Hiring is always such a bitch."

Fiona's operation was mining gold and turning it into Gold Rush? Holy fucking hell. No wonder she had her property spelled to hell and back and had been abducting people. Gold Rush was a highly addictive drug that brought on a euphoria that was unmatched by any other magical narcotic. It was notoriously hard to find because it took a powerful witch to turn the gold into the powder. I guessed Fiona was that witch.

Fuck me.

I'd also heard that gold in these mountains was deep and very dangerous to extract due to mud slides and earthquakes the mining caused below ground. The state had shut down any mining of gold in the area years ago due to the increasing dangers to not only human life, but the earth as well. There was no telling how many human lives she'd sacrificed for her greed.

"You don't seem pleased by your new accommodations, Marion," she said, intentionally trying to bait me.

"I won't be here long, so I'm not worried about it," I said, wishing feverishly that looks really could kill. I'd get out one way or another. Help would arrive shortly. I was sure of that. Brix and the coven knew where I was. And if Fiona's people hadn't gotten Charlotte and Trish, they'd be back for me, too.

"Oh, I know what you're thinking. You have people that will miss you. Ones who might even have some witchy powers." She flipped through a binder on her desk and appeared to read some notes. "Looks like you're part of a coven. Isn't that cute? I bet they could send a few pesky spells my way, but it won't take much to convince them that you and that wolf of yours ran off to find a peaceful life somewhere else. Then they'll go on with their lives and eventually no one will speak of you ever again."

"Maybe. Maybe not," I said, trying to play it cool. I had to admit that this lady could put the fear of the goddess in someone. If I had to guess, I'd say her soul was as black as midnight. The fact that she hadn't mentioned Brix or the MTF gave me some hope that she didn't know I was a part-time agent. When Brix came for me, that would mean he'd benefit from the element of surprise.

She waved to someone behind me. "Bring her in."

I twisted in my chair and swallowed a gasp when I saw Kylie being manhandled as they shoved her through the door. She was bound and gagged but still put up one hell of a fight. I desperately wanted to help her in any way I could, but since I was shackled and chained to the chair, there wasn't anything I could do.

Staring helplessly, I watched as they brought her over to Fiona.

The older woman looked Kylie up and down and then

nodded. "She's young and looks strong. I bet she does well in the mines."

"You can't send her down there!" I cried. "She has a daughter."

Fiona blinked at me and then turned her attention to Kylie. "Pay attention, Marion. You're about to see exactly how I change lives for the better."

I lurched forward as if there was something I could do to stop her, but of course the chair didn't even move an inch.

Fiona's magic sparked at her fingertips as my stomach churned.

Kylie struggled, desperately trying to get out of the guards' hands. But the moment Fiona touched her, she stilled and that vacant look I'd witnessed in Lacey's gaze overtook her.

"There, now isn't that better?" Fiona asked as she patted Kylie's hands. "Go on and find Lacey. You two have much to discuss."

Kylie blinked twice and then stared past Fiona as she said, "Oh, wow. I love lavender. I wish I had it growing on my walls at home, too."

"You will, dear," Fiona said patiently. "Or if you ever get tired of it, let us know. Some people prefer roses, others sunflowers. No request is ever too big when it comes to how you want your cabin decorated. Understand? Now go feed the wolves. They must be nice and hungry by now."

Kylie beamed at her and then let the guards guide her out of the room.

"Jax and Kai? You have them here?" I asked, already knowing the answer. She'd alluded to it earlier, but I wanted a solid confirmation.

Fiona rolled her eyes. "Of course I have them. Again, if those dumbasses would have just left me and mine alone, we wouldn't be in this mess. All I wanted was to be left in peace to run my business. But no, those two were poking around, sticking their noses where they didn't belong. I had enough of it, and now here we are. I have two pet wolves and a witch on my hands. Isn't that fun?"

"Loads of fun," I muttered.

Fiona's phone rang, and when she answered, she said, "Not now, Stone. I'm busy."

Stone. *Officer Stone?*

"No, you can't come rough her up. But you can come to the ritual tomorrow at sundown. I bet you and Wallis will get a real kick out of it."

She ended the call and looked at me. "He's not a fan of yours."

"Stone and Wallis work for you, too? Is there anyone in this town who's not on your payroll?"

She cackled. "A few have yet to sign up. But yes, Stone and Wallis get profits for cleaning up after idiots like John Vincent and taking care of busybodies like you and your sister. They do very well. Though I do have to say that I'd have ended that John character months ago if he hadn't been related to Stone's woman. I swear, I have no idea why Stone didn't let me put a bullet in his brain, but sometimes you need to keep the staff happy, am I right?"

My head was spinning. It appeared that all roads led back to Fiona and there was nothing I could do about it. At least not yet.

Fiona waved one of her guards in and said, "Take her back to her room. I have work to do." Then she turned to me. "See you tomorrow at sunset. Get your rest. It's going to be epic."

"What's tomorrow at sunset?" I asked, almost not wanting to know.

"Oh, I didn't tell you? You were right about one thing. You definitely won't be here long. Tomorrow evening is when we're burning our least favorite witch."

"Burning the witch?" I asked, my voice cracking.

Her shit-eating grin was back when she answered. "Yes. Just like the Salem Witch trials. I can't wait to see you go up in flames."

CHAPTER 25

*B*y the time sunset arrived the following day, I almost wished that Fiona had glamoured me. It would have been better than spending the last eighteen hours imagining myself going up in flames over and over and over again.

No one but Lacey and Kylie had come to visit me. And even then, all they'd done was drop off food I hadn't had the stomach to eat. Neither of them had said a word or looked me in the eye. Clearly, Fiona had ordered them to ignore me, because no amount of pleading could get them to even talk, much less get them to consider opening my cell.

I felt like an epic failure.

No one had come, and I was starting to wonder if Fiona had somehow already managed to glamour the entire coven. Had she gotten to Brix, too? At that point, I was convinced we'd all go out at the hand of the grouchy neighbor who liked card tournaments and running a multimillion-dollar drug operation. I supposed there were worst ways to go, but I couldn't think of any.

"Ready?" Fiona asked from outside my cell.

I stared the hardened old woman in the eye and said, "Yes." Anywhere was better than in my cell.

She laughed. "I do like the feisty ones. That means it's going to be very entertaining."

A guard arrived, and I was hauled out of my cell, cuffed, and strapped with chains. Then he gave me a solid push on my back and said, "Move."

Hatred curled through every fiber of my being, but I ordered myself to keep it in check. If I was going to get out of this, I was going to need every bit of my wits to keep from becoming the evening's barbeque.

"Why so glum?" Fiona taunted me as we walked from my cell and up the stairs that led to the outdoors.

I ignored her completely.

"Don't worry, you won't be cold for long." At the top of the stairs, she swept off over to a large red-velvet throne and then perched on the edge like she was the goddamned Queen of England. There were bleachers behind her that were filled with haggard-looking men and women, all of them dressed in coveralls and looking as if they hadn't showered in days. To her right were the women who were dressed in white. Both Lacey and Kylie were there. And to her left were Stone, Wallis, Sharon Krass, and John Vincent. A wolf, whom I assumed was Jessa, strolled up and sat at Fiona's feet.

I shook my head, wondering if this was all just a terrible nightmare.

But when I spotted Jax and Kai being wheeled out in

locked cages, I knew in my heart it was reality. They were both covered in dirt and blood and looked like they'd been beaten within an inch of their lives.

My heart felt as if it was breaking in two, and I couldn't help it when I called out, "Jax!"

His head jerked up, and those dark eyes I adored so much met mine. There was a world of emotion swimming in his gaze, and I supposed he must be seeing the same thing reflected back at him.

I love you, Jax mouthed to me.

Tears stung my eyes as I mouthed the same back to him.

"Oh, now isn't that sweet!" Fiona's voice boomed across the clearing. "The two lovebirds declaring their undying love for each other just before the wolf watches his witch go up in flames. Someone will be writing epic tragedies about this moment just like they did with Romeo and Juliet. If I had a heart, it'd be touched."

Jax snarled in her direction.

I just kept my focus on him, preferring to spend these last moments concentrating on someone I cared about.

"It's time to get this show started. Who's ready?" Fiona called.

No one responded until Stone stood up and started to clap with enthusiasm. And then it was as if a spell had been cast, and all of the zombie workers joined him along with Wallis, Sharon, and John.

My stomach roiled, and I prayed I didn't vomit in front of all those vile people.

"Bring her to the platform!" Fiona ordered the guard.

I planted my feet, making him all but drag me across the field. My shoes came off, and suddenly my bare feet were touching the earth. I sent all my magical concentration to the soles of my feet, trying to suck up as much of the earth's energy as I could. My magic wasn't strong without my dagger, but I had to try. I had to do something, anything, to keep from being burned to a crisp.

Tendrils of magic tingled in my feet, giving me a tiny bit of hope.

"Move," the guard ordered as he pushed me toward the wooden stairs of the structure.

I refused, instead making him carry me up as I went limp just to make his job harder. If there was one thing I was *not* going to do, it was willingly walking to my public burning.

As the guard and two of his buddies tied me to the thick wooden post, Fiona stepped behind a podium and pounded a gavel against it.

Everyone instantly went silent.

"Welcome to the public witch trial of one Marion Matched," Fiona crowed. "She is here on charges of... Well, it doesn't really matter what the charges are, now does it? This is what happens when a witch can't mind her own business. Now we're going to watch her go up in flames so we never have to deal with her brand of bullshit again." She turned to Stone and held out a torch that was already alive with fire. "Would you like to do the honors, Stone? I know how much trouble she gave you."

"I'd be honored, Fiona. Thank you." He took the torch and slowly walked toward me while the wolves behind me snarled and rattled their cages. I desperately wished I could see Jax's face at that moment. But since I couldn't, I stared

Stone down and imagined boils forming on the bottoms of his feet.

Suddenly, the police officer let out a yelp and started hopping from foot to foot. "What are you doing to me, you fucking witch?!" He dropped to his knees, and I shifted my focus to his legs. He screamed and rolled over, dropping the torch as he writhed in agony. Intense satisfaction filled me, and I went for the jugular. With my gaze laser-focused on his crotch, I imagined his entire groin covered in pubic lice.

His hand instantly reached between his legs, and he started scratching aggressively.

I couldn't help the small bark of laughter that escaped my lips.

"You whore!" Sharon ran from her seat, picked up the still burning torch, and threw it into the pit below my platform.

There was a *whoosh* sound, and the boards beneath my feet instantly warmed.

"Fuck," I muttered.

"That's what you get for harassing me," Sharon said before she spit on me.

I glared at her, and this time when I stared at her crotch, I imagined genital herpes.

She let out a yelp and ran out of the clearing toward the house.

"That's enough, Marion. I think you've had plenty of fun for one day, though I admire your tenacity. It's too bad I didn't find you a good fit for this operation," Fiona said, and then she reached up and pinched her fingers together.

My magic fled, leaving me feeling completely defenseless. The heat below the platform was becoming almost unbearable, and sweat was pouring from my forehead, blinding my vision. I closed my eyes and silently prayed for it all to end sooner rather than later. But then I heard Jax calling my name, and I jerked my head up just in time to see a rush of people suddenly appear inside the clearing.

My sister Charlotte was there in front of me, the dagger in her hand as tears ran down her face. She called, "Don't give up on me now, Marion!"

Then the dagger I'd carried around with me for months was suddenly in one of my hands. A rush of power flowed into my hand and filled my entire system until I was vibrating with it. I had the dagger, and in theory, I should have been able to cut the ropes binding me to the pole, but the angle was too awkward and would take too long. If I tried to manually cut them, I'd be burning before I even got through the first strand.

I needed a new plan.

One that involved all the supercharged magic churning inside of me. Closing my eyes while trying to ignore the lick of flames starting to claim my feet and ankles, I pictured the gorgeous blue lagoon that Jax and I had found on a hike earlier that summer. It had been surrounded by rock outcroppings, and a waterfall spilled from the far side, giving it a magical quality. With that image firmly in my mind's eye, I imagined that in place of the fire below the platform. And then I remembered the rain shower that had drenched us just as we were thinking about hiking back to the trailhead.

The memory of our laughter filled my senses, and suddenly I cried, "Goddess of the clouds, make it rain!"

Magic shot into the sky from the dagger I still held in my hand. And just like that, the sky opened up and rain came down in sheets, dousing the last of the flames that clung to the rickety platform.

I blinked through the rain and smiled when I realized the area right in front of my platform had turned into the gorgeous blue lagoon that would be forever seared into my memory.

"Marion?" my sister Charlotte said into my ear.

I jerked my head to the side and spotted her frantically trying to cut through my ropes with the dagger.

"I've got this," I said, my voice scratchy and weak. "Let me have the dagger again."

She didn't question me as she pressed it back into my hand.

All it took was one clear thought of the ropes coming undone for them to fall from my body, freeing me.

"Oh my gods," Charlotte sobbed as she wrapped her arms around me. "I thought for sure you were a goner."

I let out a humorless laugh and said, "Me too."

When she pulled away, I looked around at the complete chaos that surrounded us and stared opened-mouthed at the cavalry she had brought along with her. Brix was there, fighting Fiona, each of them trading magical barb to magical barb. Two wolves were mauling each other. Jax had Stone on the ground as he threw blow after blow at the cop's face. Trish was ushering Lacey and Kylie away from the mayhem while snarling in the direction of Fiona. And then there was the coven. They had formed a circle around the area Fiona had constructed for my witch burning, and they were doing a neutralization spell to weaken the magic that Fiona seemed to be wielding. It was working too, because Brix finally had her in a headlock and the magic streaming off her started to sputter.

"Come on," Charlotte said. "Let's get you out of here."

"Not without Jax," I said.

She let out a sigh but didn't stop me when I hurried over to him.

"I think—" I started but was knocked over by Officer Wallis.

Jax shouted at him but then fielded a blow from Stone and went back to beating the crap out of him.

I got to my feet, grabbed Wallis's arm, and then twisted. There was still an overload of magic in my system, so when I yanked his arm to the right, the man flipped all the way over and landed with his face in the dirt. I immediately pounced and was surprised when someone passed me a couple of magical zip ties. I glanced to see Charlotte shaking her head at me. "Thank you," I told her and then finished securing Wallis.

"Nice job," Jax said as I climbed off the man.

I turned, noting that Stone was also tied up, and then threw myself into Jax's arms.

"I thought we both might be done for there for a minute," he said into my ear.

"You and me both." There was a sob in my voice, but I swallowed it and hung on for dear life.

"It's over now, Marion. You're safe," Jax said.

"And so are you." I held him tighter and vowed to never let go.

CHAPTER 26

"Look at all these articles about you," Aunt Lucy said as she slapped them down on my kitchen table. It was Saturday night, and even though I'd been captured and nearly burned alive earlier in the week, I'd insisted on cooking the family dinner we'd planned. All I'd wanted to do since Jax and I had gotten home was spend time with those I loved.

"That's an article about Brix," I said after glancing at it. He'd been quite the celebrity since the epic takedown of Fiona and her crew. The town paper had run article after article, hailing him as our town hero.

"It's calling you the Rainmaker Witch," she said, beaming with pride. "I still wish I'd been there to see that."

"No you don't," Charlotte said, nudging her aside so she could set the table. "It was awful, and I thought we were going to lose Marion, Aunt Lucy. I know it sounds badass and everything—"

"It *was* badass. And so are you, Char-Char," Aunt Lucy said as she patted Charlotte's cheek.

My sister's nostrils flared, and I knew she was getting annoyed. "Yes, Charlotte was badass. If she hadn't figured out how to supercharge the dagger with the coven's magic, this all would have ended quite differently."

As it turned out, Charlotte and Trish had gotten away the night I'd fallen into the pit. They'd immediately gone for help, first trying Brix and then the coven. Brix had still been unreachable, but the coven had immediately pulled together and helped her come up with an ambush. They'd just gotten to Fiona's on the night of the burning when Brix showed up and let them lead the mission, acting as backup.

In the end, he'd taken down Fiona while the coven had done considerable damage to her magic. It had been a complete team effort, and that's the way the press had written it early on, but now they had a fixation with Brix. It seemed the entire female population of Premonition Pointe had decided he was the hero they wanted to date.

I thought it was hilarious. He was just embarrassed.

"We got another two dozen calls at the agency today for someone who looks like Brix," Charlotte said over her shoulder. "Are you sure he doesn't want us to fix him up with someone?"

I let out a chuckle. "Nope. No matter how many times I ask, he says he doesn't need help in the dating department."

"That's too bad," she said, shaking her head. "Imagine the publicity we could have generated by posting about his dating adventures."

"That would have been something," I agreed as I slipped my arm around Jax. "But it doesn't matter. Now that all these articles are coming out, suddenly no one remembers we're the agency who repped a murder suspect, and everyone wants a Brix or Jax or Kai of their own."

"Gonna be hard to give them one of us, since the other two have sworn off dating and I'm very much taken," Jax said.

"True," I said. "But that's why Charlotte and I are the best. We'll still find them alphas of their own."

Charlotte whipped around and stared at me. "Did you mean that? The Charlotte part, I mean?"

"Yes. Absolutely." I grinned at her.

"Does that mean I get a raise?" she asked with one eyebrow cocked.

I threw my head back and laughed. "We'll talk about it next week, but as long as business starts picking back up, I think that's doable."

"Well then," she said, beaming. "Let me just say you're the best sister and boss a girl could ever have."

I let go of Jax and went to give her a hug. We held on longer than necessary and didn't pull apart until I heard my father say, "There's my two best girls. How's it feel to be heroes?"

"We're not heroes, Dad," Charlotte said as she went back into the kitchen to help get the food on the table.

"Sure you are. Because of you that nasty Fiona and her two dirty cops are gonna spend the rest of their lives behind bars. Mining gold and turning it into Gold Rush, plus abducting innocent people, those are major offenses. And they are looking at multiple counts each," he said and then added, "Can you believe anyone actually fell for that crazy lady Fiona's BS down at the card tournament? I knew the moment I met her that something was off."

"No you didn't!" Aunt Lucy cried, and the two started bickering.

I imagined my aunt was correct. Fiona had glamoured a lot of people besides the ones she had working at her drug factory. There was also the mother down at Chick-A-Daze farm as well as everyone else at that card tournament. My father just hated being made to look like a fool. And no matter how many times I told him it didn't reflect on him, he was going to go to his grave insisting he wasn't fooled by Fiona.

I turned to Jax. "Have you heard from Kai?"

He frowned. "Kai isn't coming."

"I was afraid of that." During the take down of Fiona and the crew, Kai had been in a dirty battle with Jessa that had ended Jessa's life. It had been an open and shut case of self-defense as Jessa was about to rip Kai's throat out, but it still had left him pretty messed up. As much as he hated her for what she'd done to him, he did love her at one time. I imagined he'd be working through those emotions for quite a while. "I just hope he's not alone."

"Trish is with him," Jax said. "She's staying in a small cabin out near the woods, and in exchange she's doing some work in the office for him. She told me they were having dinner together, and she keeps an eye on him just to make sure he has someone around to talk to when he needs it."

I let out a sigh of relief. "Good. That means I'll worry less about both of them."

"Me, too," he said and kissed the top of my head. "Oh, Brix called earlier. He said that Lacey and Kylie have been detoxed, and after some deprograming, they'll be reunited with their children next week."

"Thank the gods." Even Sharon had been arrested. It turned out that she'd been cooking Fiona's books for years. As for her brother John, there hadn't been any actual evidence that he'd been involved in the drug making or trafficking, but he had been caught with an unregistered weapon and was currently serving time for breaking the terms of his restraining order. It appeared that everything was right again in Premonition Pointe.

Everything except for that spa appointment I'd missed. Earlier that day, Charlotte had already given me hell for the gray streak in my red hair and then pointed out the couple of whiskers on my chin. It had taken all my effort not to kick her out of the house. Instead, I'd spent some quality time with my tweezers and some temporary dye, and then I made a new appointment for next week. It was a start.

Ty and Kennedy arrived, and ten minutes later we were all seated at the table, ready to dig into the lasagna I'd baked. Dinner was lively as we all talked over each other while Minx and Paris Francine did their best to get the attention of anyone who would give them nibbles.

I sat back and admired the scene as laughter filled my small house. It was something I'd cherished before, but now after staring death in the face, it meant the world to me to have each and every one of them there in that moment.

I was watching Kennedy tease Ty about the sauce left on his face when the sound of a utensil tapping on a water glass got my attention. I glanced up and nearly fell out of my chair when I spotted Jax standing and holding a black-velvet box in his hand. "Jax?"

"Marion," he said as he lowered himself, bending to one knee.

"Oh my gods. This is really happening, isn't it?" I said, barely able to breathe.

"I know this is sooner than we talked about, but after what happened at Fiona's, I—"

"Yes!" I shouted as tears trickled down my face.

"Yes?" Jax asked. "I didn't even ask you anything yet."

"No, but you were going to, and the answer is yes." I beamed, staring into his gorgeous dark eyes.

"It's been thirty years in the making," he said with a chuckle as he gently wrapped his fingers around my left hand. "So forgive me if I want to do this right. Marion Matched, will you do me the extreme pleasure of marrying me?"

I reached out and cupped his cheek with my free hand. "Jax Williams, it would be the honor of my life. Yes."

Jax slipped the most brilliant square cut diamond ring onto my finger and then pulled me up and into his arms. And right there, in front of all the people we loved best, we sealed our engagement with a kiss.

CHAPTER 27

SIX MONTHS LATER

"The house is beautiful," Charlotte said as she laced up my corset dress. "It's a damned miracle it was done in time though."

I nodded as I tried not to wince and cursed myself for not spending more time on the treadmill. The dress fit, but breathing was going to be a bit of a challenge. The house in question was the one that Jax had built for us on the beachfront property he'd purchased the year before. After our engagement, he'd made it a priority to get it done. He'd said it was my wedding present, but I knew he just wanted a place that was ours once we were hitched.

"Oh my gosh," Charlotte said softly. "You look amazing, Marion."

"I do?" I shifted to stand in front of the mirror and was amazed by the transformation. My waist was cinched, my hair had been put into a fancy updo with some soft curls framing my face, and my makeup looked like a professional had done it. In reality, it had been Charlotte. Her talents never ceased to amaze me.

"Are you ready yet?" Celia asked impatiently from the other side of the mirror.

It didn't even surprise me anymore when she popped in. "Is everyone here?"

"Yep. Even Kai Gray." She pumped her eyebrows as if there was some gossip behind that fact.

"Okay, I'll bite," Charlotte said. "Why are you making that face?"

"Because he's the most eligible bachelor here, and everyone, and I do mean everyone, seems to want him," she said, her eyes gleaming.

"Including you?" I asked.

"No. I'm taken," she said with a huff. "Though I would enjoy that challenge."

I frowned at her. "I thought you said he was boring?"

She just shrugged. "That was before I realized how enjoyable it is to watch him work out. No one else has a body like that." Celia gave us an exaggerated wink and then disappeared again.

I walked over to the window of my master bedroom and looked down at the guests that were already seated and waiting for the ceremony to start. Sure enough, Kai was there, sitting by himself in the back row. But I didn't miss his gaze lingering on Autumn.

"Those two are still perfect for each other," Charlotte said.

"I know, but Kai doesn't want to date, and I won't fix her up with someone who is so closed off," I said.

"A more motivated matchmaker would figure out how

to get them in the same room together until they realized how hot they are for each other. You know, like a closet at a wedding reception."

"Charlotte, please tell me you're not planning something like that," I pleaded.

"Oops, look at the time," she said, ignoring my comment. "You don't want to be late to marry the man of your dreams, do you?"

I opened my mouth to protest but then heard the wedding song playing, indicating it was indeed time to meet Jax at the altar.

The door opened and my dad walked in. His eyes were misty as he held his arm out to me. I took it, and when we stepped outside onto the carpet that led to the altar on the gazebo, I beamed at the love of my life, ready to promise him forever.

DEANNA'S BOOK LIST

<u>Witches of Keating Hollow:</u>
Soul of the Witch
Heart of the Witch
Spirit of the Witch
Dreams of the Witch
Courage of the Witch
Love of the Witch
Power of the Witch
Essence of the Witch
Muse of the Witch
Vision of the Witch
Waking of the Witch
Honor of the Witch
Promise of the Witch
Return of the Witch
Fortune of the Witch
Song of the Witch

Keating Hollow Happily Ever Afters:
Gift of the Witch
Wisdom of the Witch
Light of the Witch

Witches of Befana Bay:
The Witch's Silver Lining
The Witch's Secret Love
The Witch's Lost Spell

Witches of Christmas Grove:
A Witch For Mr. Holiday
A Witch For Mr. Christmas
A Witch For Mr. Winter
A Witch For Mr. Mistletoe
A Witch For Mr. Frost
A Witch For Mr. Garland

Premonition Pointe Novels:
Witching For Grace
Witching For Hope
Witching For Joy
Witching For Clarity
Witching For Moxie
Witching For Kismet
Witching For Autumn

Miss Matched Midlife Dating Agency:
Star-crossed Witch
Honor-bound Witch
Outmatched Witch

Moonstruck Witch
Rainmaker Witch

Jade Calhoun Novels:
Haunted on Bourbon Street
Witches of Bourbon Street
Demons of Bourbon Street
Angels of Bourbon Street
Shadows of Bourbon Street
Incubus of Bourbon Street
Bewitched on Bourbon Street
Hexed on Bourbon Street
Dragons of Bourbon Street

Pyper Rayne Novels:
Spirits, Stilettos, and a Silver Bustier
Spirits, Rock Stars, and a Midnight Chocolate Bar
Spirits, Beignets, and a Bayou Biker Gang
Spirits, Diamonds, and a Drive-thru Daiquiri Stand
Spirits, Spells, and Wedding Bells

Ida May Chronicles:
Witched To Death
Witch, Please
Stop Your Witchin'

Crescent City Fae Novels:
Influential Magic
Irresistible Magic
Intoxicating Magic

Last Witch Standing:
Bewitched by Moonlight
Soulless at Sunset
Bloodlust By Midnight
Bitten At Daybreak

Witch Island Brides:
The Wolf's New Year Bride
The Vampire's Last Dance
The Warlock's Enchanted Kiss
The Shifter's First Bite

Destiny Novels:
Defining Destiny
Accepting Fate

Wolves of the Rising Sun:
Jace
Aiden
Luc
Craved
Silas
Darien
Wren

Black Bear Outlaws:
Cyrus
Chase
Cole

<u>Bayou Springs Alien Mail Order Brides:</u>

Zeke

Gunn

Echo

ABOUT THE AUTHOR

New York Times and USA Today bestselling author, Deanna Chase, is a native Californian, transplanted to the slower paced lifestyle of southeastern Louisiana. When she isn't writing, she is often goofing off with her husband in New Orleans or playing with her two shih tzu dogs. For more information and updates on newest releases visit her website at deannachase.com.

www.ingramcontent.com/pod-product-compliance
Lightning Source LLC
Chambersburg PA
CBHW022109240626
47153CB00007B/2291